Skin & Bone

Novels also by the author:

The (D)Evolution of Us
Glasshouse
Underrated

Cover Your Tracks

Morwenna Blackwood

To Lee Dickinson

Acknowledgements (original from first edition)

Although I'd written the first draft of this novel long before the programme was aired, I'd like to thank Sir David Attenborough and the BBC for their incredible documentary, *Dinosaurs: The Final Day*. It had a profound effect on me and influenced my edits of Skin and Bone.

Thanks to my writer friends, Jenny Kane and PJ Reed, for their input about how best to murder someone with an archaeology tool, and their continued camaraderie and support!

Thanks as ever to Phil and to Dad, and of course to Laurence and Steph and the darkstroke community.

But mostly, thanks to my little boy, K, for rekindling my love of dinosaurs and palaeontology. Things have come a long way since the 1980s, and I've learnt – and am still learning – loads! 'What's the chorus?'...!

About the Author

When Morwenna Blackwood was six years old, she got told off for filling a school exercise book with a seemingly endless story, when she should have been listening to the teacher/eating her tea/colouring with her friends. The story was about a frog. It never did end; and Morwenna never looked back.

Born and raised in Devon, Morwenna suffered from severe OCD and depression, and spent her childhood and teens in libraries. She travelled about for a decade before returning to the West Country. She now has an MA in Creative Writing, and has written several novels, short stories, and a collection of poetry. When she is not writing, she works for an animal rescue charity, or can be found down by the sea.

She often thinks about that frog.

Skin & Bone

Eskwich, Autumn 2019

Richard

"Exactly what planet are you on, *mate*?! You don't get to hold a knife to my friend's throat and then sit down and have a drink with me! You get to fuck off! And give your dad a call – his cat died yesterday."

I've not been in The Riverboat for years, but nothing's changed. Well, I say nothing's changed, but I suppose quite a lot *has* changed for a little backwater town like this. The place has been bought out by Wetherspoons and suffered a fifteen-minute make-over, which basically means they've chucked a load of beige paint around the place, taken out the pool table and the jukebox, and been to B & M for some new furniture. It also means that Stuart, who's been bar manager the whole time I've lived – or owned the maisonette at least – here, has now got to wear what passes for a uniform: black shirt, black trousers, black shiny shoes and a name badge instead of his battered jeans, checked shirt and Converse trainers. And there are more bottles of gin on the shelves than shots. Oh, and people openly pull knives on each other at the bar these days, instead of just taking it outside and trying to knock each other out. And they call this the 'snowflake 'generation!

I've come back to the West Country to check that the scummy tenants have actually left my maisonette, and if they have, to do the inevitable clear-up. It turned out to be a good move, putting the place up for rent while I was in Liverpool instead of just selling up: partly for the income, and partly because I still had a base near my dear brother, Adam, and, after all, I suppose this shithole of a town has changed my life, made a man out of me, if you like. Also, it's an easy drive to the Jurassic Coast, Lyme Regis, and Kilve on the north coast; it's also a good place to stop on the way to the Isle of Wight.

I dumped my stuff off at my place on Angel Hill and

walked the short distance down to my brother's bike shop. I wasn't expecting a warm welcome, but I thought the ice might have thawed enough over the years for Adam and me to be able to have a drink together and chat about old times. I walked into the little shop, as ever, packed to the rafters with bikes and bike paraphernalia, and stinking of oil and metal. Adam was at the counter, fiddling about with a bit of chain, or something, and when I said *hello*, he'd replied with, *Fuck off, Richard. My cat's just died.* So I fucked off to the only place worth fucking off to – The Riverboat.

I had to stick up for Stuart, though. He did give me a job all those years ago when I was released from Channings Wood. Must be twenty-odd years ago, now! I only referred to him as my 'friend', because 'acquaintance 'wouldn't have had enough clout, and I sure as hell wasn't going to call him my 'boss'!

This lad – I kind of recognised him, but he must only have been in his early twenties – obviously had some beef with Stuart. I clocked that from the moment I walked up to the bar. Stuart had just slammed the guy's pint down in front of him so hard that some of it had slopped onto his phone. In my opinion, this was the lad's fault. You don't leave your phone on the bar – anyone could nick it! But then he was pissed. He was leaning on the bar, all fitted Superdry t-shirt, jeans with the turn-ups that reached halfway up his calf, giving you the retch-inducing view of his bare ankles sticking out of his white trainers like pale, hairy pins.

"Fucking coke-head cunt!" he spat at Stuart, wiping his phone on his jeans. "First you come on to my girlfriend, then you try to trash my phone!"

"Leave it out, son," Stuart said. He couldn't have sounded any more condescending if he'd tried. "Your *girlfriend* owes me. And anymore of that language and I'll get Security to remove you from the premises. In fact, I'd be doing your mum and dad a favour if I just called them over now – after all, it is a school night –"

Suddenly the lad had Stuart by his collar and pulled a flick-knife out of his pocket! It was brilliant! I hadn't had this level of entertainment in a pub for years! Stuart said, "Back off, Liam!" And that's when it hit me who the boy was: my long, lost nephew! Little Liam, who'd been a blond toddler the last time I'd clapped eyes on him!

I was having such fun watching them that I laughed, and the lad whipped his head round to me. As soon as he saw my face, the daggers in his eyes turned to those pulsing hearts, or stars like you get in cartoons, and he said, still holding the knife to Stuart's throat, "Oh my God! You're that guy on the telly! You did that dinosaur documentary on BBC2 with Chris Packham! Wow! What you said about spinosaurids blew my mind! Can I get you a drink, mate?" I said what I said. There was a pause. Then, "Do I know you from somewhere?"

Portia

The low cliffs are layered like Liquorice Allsorts. Liam's stumbling over terrain which is literally just rocks and boulders, slipping on seaweed in his chequered espadrilles in pursuit of Richard.

"Liam! Just leave it!" I scream from what feels like miles away. I can't be more than a few metres behind him, but I can barely keep upright. I've never seen a beach like this in my life.

Liam's been on about coming here ever since he started uni. Everyone knows that you can sometimes find fossils in Lyme Regis, and possibly other beaches along the Jurassic Coast – we've been to Lyme loads, and if we're at a south coast beach it's always Orcombe Point – but like I say, he didn't know about Kilve until he went to uni. And then there was never time when he came back in the holidays because he was always working; I mean, like, *always* working. In the olden days, if you went to uni, the government gave you a student grant and a loan that hardly anyone ever bothered paying back, but now you have a choice between not going and working your bollocks off; going, and getting into massive debt; or going and working your fucking bollocks off. Liam chose the latter. He's finished his first degree at Liverpool now, but he'll be starting a Masters in Manchester in October. Palaeontology. He'll discover a new dinosaur; I know he will. Or find a bit of the meteor that killed them. From what he's said, I think that's really what he wants to do. Like, find proof it actually happened. Unearthing the past is his passion, literally *and* metaphorically. But when he asked me to come to Kilve with him today, I thought he was going to propose to me – put a diamond ring inside an ammonite and let me 'find 'it, or something – not use me as back-up or a witness or something while he confronted his uncle

Richard!

I don't even know how he knew Richard would be here today. We never talked about him. I only knew about him when Liam's grandad got dementia and we had to go and clear his house out when he had to go into a home. We found these old photos. Some were of Liam's mum, Kayleigh, who got murdered by some psycho; some were of her and his dad and their friends when they were our age. I'd said something like, *Wow, Liam! Who s that dark haired guy? He s gorgeous!* and Liam had glanced at a photo and told me it was Richard. I'd said he looked like his Uncle Richard, except he had his mum's eyes – which was just a statement of fact - and Liam had said I'd made him sound like some fucked-up Harry Potter.

He'd looked at me with a vitriol that'd scared me. It was the only time I'd seen Liam like that, so I kept quiet. He only told me about Richard and what he'd done, a few weeks later when he was pissed up. After that, we never mentioned his uncle again.

And now he's chasing Richard down on a beach full of fossils. My instinct is to call the police, but I don't want to get Liam into trouble, and nothing more than words has happened, anyway.

"Liam!" I shout again.

This time he turns and stops. "Fuck's sake, Portia! That's not helpful! Go back to the car!"

Richard is a fair distance in front of him, now. He's been here before – he's using a bit of branch from the woods to steady himself. Liam starts off again, but stumbles and crashes onto his knees. "Fuck!" He scrambles to his feet, grabs a large stone and hurls it at Richard. It skims his uncle's heel, and shatters on a long, grey platform of rock. Richard spins round, laughing soullessly, his face harsh with triumph. It looks like he's going to spit at Liam, but his eyes fall to the rock, and he suddenly softens and drops into a crouch. He picks up one of the fragments of the stone

Liam threw and examines it as he stands. In the hiatus, I pick my way, half walking, half climbing, to Liam, and grab his hand. Liam is as cold and still as the sloping shelf of rock we're standing on.

"Liam?" I whisper. It might be that I've just noticed the wind off the sea, but I'm suddenly very cold.

"It's an ammonite."

"What?"

"There's an ammonite imprint on that stone I threw."

"So?"

"It's been here for millions of years, and I've just thrown it like it's nothing."

Richard is picking up other bits of the stone now, turning them over and over in his hands. He seems oblivious to us.

"So?"

"Richard just got tenure. In the palaeontology department."

As if he's heard his nephew's mumble, Richard stares right at us. He's livid. He cocks his head to one side and pierces us with his gaze.

"Liam?" My hand scrabbles for his.

Richard picks up a boulder like it's a pebble. He's stronger than he looks. Without taking his eyes from Liam's, he walks towards us, oblivious to the severe landscape.

"You stupid little prick."

Richard is so close to us now that I can smell the alcohol on his breath, the sweat that's soaked through his t-shirt. Liam and I can't move. I can't look at Liam, because I am so scared of Richard, but I know he's paralysed, like me.

"Your mum was a good shag," Richard tells Liam, his head still on one side - he looks psychopathic - "even when she wasn't up for it. Now you finally get to meet her."

He smashes the rock into the side of Liam's head.

Kilve, January 2022

Liam

Agony. My arm protests as I move it to the source of the pain. My hand comes away from my temple, bloody. I'm shivering. My feet are wet, and I don't know why. I decide to open my eyes and am surprised to find that they are already open – it's just pitch black. A sudden coldness seeps up from my feet to my knees. I can smell salt. I'm in the water. I'm in the sea! I need to get out of the sea! My head pounds as I try to lift it. My whole body throbs. I can hardly see a thing, but my eyes are adjusting; the clouds don't quite cover the sky, so there's a bit of silver light. I try to stand, and immediately collapse. It feels like my knees are cut. Panic and bile rise in me. I manage to turn my head to the side before I vomit. My stomach and chest heave. When I'm empty and my eyes have stopped watering, I half crawl, half drag myself away from the noise of the sea. Then it hits me. Where's Richard? And where's Portia?!

Portia

"Oh my God, Porche, it's not that I don't want to come home and see you – I'm literally not allowed! It's against the law!" Liam's exasperated, but so am I! This whole situation is crazy!

"But you haven't got Covid! Just put a mask on and get on a train! If anyone asks you, say it's an emergency!"

"You're not listening, Porche! Look – I love you! You know I do! Christ, not many people stay together when one of them goes to uni -"

"Yeah, but we're not 'many people'! And if you'd have just come home like everyone else did when they knew the restrictions were coming in, we wouldn't be in this position now!"

I'm stomping up and down in front of the bird-shit covered statue of Edward the Peacemaker. I don't know what he did, except make peace somehow. I could do with some tips. I shouldn't really be out, but I'm going mental stuck in the house with Mum and Dad all day. It's bad enough normally, but this third lockdown is a fucking killer. If I get questioned, I'll just say I'm out for my daily exercise – I'm still in town, and they can't tell me how far I can walk from my house. On the bridge on the other side of the road, there are a couple of kids from school, kissing. They're virtually outside the police station, and no one's telling them off. This is bullshit! Realisation smacks me in the face.

"You're shagging that Atlanta, or whatever she calls herself, aren't you?!"

Liam snaps back. "I think you mean Atlantis, *Porche.* And her real name is Georgia."

Georgia. At least my nickname makes sense! The wind picks up, and I get showered with fat drops of rain and some leaves. An old conker shell blows off the grass and hits my boot. If I painted it red, it would look like the Covid atom, or whatever it is. They show it on the news all the time. In the extended pause – I won't say 'pregnant 'because we had a near-miss the last time Liam was down – I pick it up and lob it in the river.

I want to believe he loves me, but he wasn't up for us getting a tattoo that time, and I've seen this Georgia in pictures on Liam's Instagram. She's gorgeous, and she's always got one arm wrapped around a bloke. She's got shellacked nails, and false eyelashes, and she's probably had a boob job, too … I stop myself mid-rage. She's probably lovely, and she probably has to deal with this hate stuff all the time. But I'm jealous – she's known him five minutes and she gets to share a house with him, when I wanted to move up to Liverpool with him when he went, but he said I should finish at Exeter College, first. I know he was right, but it still pisses me off. I'm stuck with my parents, while he could be doing anything up there and I wouldn't know! The only good thing about Covid is that I've studied harder than I normally would have, just to stave off the boredom, and I'm really hoping to get the grades so I can go up and do History – if Boris ever lets us out.

Liam sighs. We do this a lot these days. We can spend over an hour on the phone, mostly in silence.

"I love you," I say, unable to keep the desperation out of my voice. I know you can't make a relationship work just with words – willing it into being – but what else have we got?

"Lee, you utter ledge!" A bloke shouts in the background over Liam's phone, and it sounds like he's just slapped him on the back.

There's a rustle, and I know Liam's putting his phone against his shoulder, redundantly, like he does when he doesn't want to be heard. I clearly hear him say, "I'm on the phone a minute, mate, but I'll have one of those if you're offering!"

Then to me he says, "Sorry, Porche. I know this is hard, but I do love you too, you know." Ordinarily this would be touching, but I hear him crack the can of lager or cider or whatever it is, open, so it feels like a slap in the face.

"Yeah. Whatevs," I spit, stabbing my finger on the red button and shoving the phone back into my bag.

The tears come as soon as my hand leaves the phone. This is so fucking hard. It's like that old Coldplay song I heard playing in someone's flat on the way here – *The Scientist.* At least it wasn't bloody Ed Sheeran. I turn my back on grimy old do-gooder, Edward, on the river and on the town and head back home. The long way round.

The only reason I know it's Saturday, is because it said so on my phone. The days are blurring again, and even though it's cold, I'd rather be outside than in because at least nature hasn't stopped. The wind's still blowing; the birds are still flying about; the hedgehogs are still getting run over. I wonder how 'essential 'the journey that killed it, was. I wonder what it was doing up and about so early in the year. Whatever, it's in the road in front of the school, and it's dead, so I guess it's a moot point. I sit on the playground fence of Wilcombe Primary School. I went there when I was a kid. There's no one about – obviously - but I can hear kids laughing and shouting and crying from inside their houses. Bugger being a mum – it looks like bloody hard work to me. A couple of crows land and poke at the hedgehog. It wasn't a wasted journey for the driver or the spikey little guy: life goes on. I watch them and toke on my vape. The sweet-scented smoke billows around me and I wish I could just disappear into it and drift away. Or Abracadabra myself out of here.

The building opposite me is Sunningmead Community Centre. It used to be a school. Around the reception area are six massive terracotta tubs, each home to a rotting sunflower. Someone must have put them there last summer, thinking that everything was returning to normal.

And now they're dead, and no one's cleared them away. Unless it's an environmental thing, and they're hoping the birds will eat the seeds. Why have seeds when you can have a dead hedgehog? Unless the gardener's dead from Covid. Fuck. We're all going to hell in a handbag. Having said that, I've switched to vaping because it's healthier, and I don't want to die of lung cancer. Ugh.

I take another drag and enjoy the warmth of the as it goes down. I'm trying custard flavour because they didn't have any rhubarb left. The guy on the till in the corner shop laughed, but it made perfect sense to me. Actually he was pretty fit, and I'm sure he looked at me in that way. It's incredible how much wearing a facemask accentuates the eyes. But I guess that if that's all you've got to go on, you fix on it. Which brings me back to Liam - all we have at the moment are words, but they're never enough. Not when you fancy someone like I fancy Liam.

Kilve, January 2022

Richard

One blow to the temple, and Liam's down. I take him out first, because what's a stick-thin girl in skin-tight jeans and heeled boots going to do? Her phone's clearly visible in her back pocket – in fact it's half sticking out - but there's no way she's going to get a 999 call off in time. I've even got time to pause when Liam hits the stones. He's so young and perfect. I can still see him as a baby, even if his hair's dark now. Like mine. He's my nephew, and the nearest thing I've got to a kid, as far as I know, but he wilfully smashed up something that's survived 200 million years! Cause and effect, if not quite an eye for an eye. Unless he dies, but I don't think he will. I didn't hit him that hard. He'll either be okay, or he won't; and if he is, then what better way to show him who's in control? And if I take the girl, then he'll have to help me. Either way, it's win-win for me, and a modicum of justice for the ammonite.

Portia hasn't moved. You get the measure of someone in their reactions to crisis situations. She's barely even looked at her darling boyfriend! She's looking at me – her crimson lips are frozen in an O. It's very alluring.

"You're coming back with me. I'll show you my tools. I could teach you to use them. Then we'll go on a nice little holiday to the Isle of Wight. With or without your lover. How does that sound?"

Liam

My dad's place is an absolute shithole, but the cat doesn't seem to mind. Dad bloody dotes on that cat, who he's imaginatively named, Shadow. It's not even ironic – Shadow is black. Dad works all the hours under the sun trying to keep Grumfer's bike shop open, and when he comes home, all he wants to do is lose himself in a four pack of cider and binge-watch stuff on Netflix, Shadow curled up on his lap. *Netflix and chill* literally means Netflix and chill for Dad. To be fair, they have some good series on, and sometimes I wish Porche would just let me watch. I'm up half the night watching the bits we missed when we were supposedly watching it together. I know I should be thankful – half my mates say their girlfriends go off sex after the first six months, like a six-month itch instead of seven-year one – but sometimes I literally can't be fucked with it. She's into all this weird stuff, too, like if she's not reading about ancient civilisations, she's reading these *X* books. I've told her she doesn't have to do any of that for me, that I'm happy just doing normal stuff, but she calls me *vanilla boy* and says I need to experiment a bit, because you only live once. At least I've got her out of saying *YOLO*.

She's right, though – you do only live once. Poor old Grumfer's been diagnosed with dementia, and he's had to go into a home. It's fucking horrible. He worked all his life – he taught pretty much everyone to ride a bike, including my dad – and people loved him, and now he doesn't even know who I am. It was the saddest day of my life when I walked into his front room (he was still in his house, next door to the bike shop) with the packet of Golden V he'd asked me to pick up for him, and he looked at me, looked at Dad, and asked him *who s that kind young man?*

"Dad, it's my boy, Liam. Your grandson," Dad said.

I heard the anguish in Dad's voice, so I said, "It's me, Grumfer! I got you your pouch of baccy and your paper. You just sent me out for it." I walked over, sat down on the arm of the sofa next to his chair, and held the baccy out to him.

"'Grumfer'?! I'm not your 'Grumfer', lad!" His face showed anger, but also fear, and he turned to Dad. "Adam! I don't know who this young 'un thinks he is, but get him out of my house!" Grumfer turned on me, "Oi! I don't know who you think you are, but get out of my house! Go on! Get the fuck out!"

I rushed to the door, tears already streaming down my face. It killed me that he had killed me, without meaning to. Grumfer had been the one person who made things better. Dad and I sat up drinking beer half the night, knowing that in the morning, we'd have to start looking into nursing homes, or 'supported living', or whatever they call it. Wondering how on earth we'd clear his house out, and what we'd do with the shop. With hindsight, these things would be the least of his problems.

Richard

She's just standing there, with her mouth all red and open like that, in an O, so I kiss her. That brings her to life – not quite in the way I'd usually like, but at least it animates her. She shudders, lets out a little muffled groan, and even tries to push me away. Promising! She tastes all sweet and smoky – she vapes! I wonder what else she does. I pick her up and sling her over my shoulder. She's lighter than a sack of spuds. I let out a little laugh – it's funny that phrase should have come to mind, because I actually know that she's lighter than a sack of spuds, because I used to heave them around when I worked on the fruit and veg department in Tesco.

I'm expecting her to scream or pound my back with her fists, but she just hangs there. Disappointing.

She fits so perfectly on my shoulder, I could wear her like a scarf. The old grey matter's on fire today – it's coming up with things that make me laugh! Ah, I knew it was going to be an interesting day! I reach back with my left hand and pull Portia around. Her pretty face is now right in mine. Her cute little snub nose touches my cheek. It's wet, like a dog's. I can smell the vape smoke in her hair. I lick her face. It's salty, but I can't tell whether it's tears or just the sea air. She whimpers. Like a dog.

I know all about fear responses – fight, flight, freeze – but even my dead fiancée, Cath, wasn't this limp! How do I manage to surround myself with all these weak women? Well, I suppose this one's a girl, really. But then Cath and her mate, Kayleigh, were younger than this one, the first time.

"Can't you at least scream, or something?"

The words are out almost before I've realised I'm speaking. Portia whimpers again. We've reached the river. It's fast-flowing, without banks. Just clean, clean water rushing over ancient stones.

"Oh, for goodness 'sake!"

I unwind her and place her on the stones. Another laugh escapes me when I see the surprise on her face.

"I'm not going to hurt you, Portia," I tell her. She makes to run off, which makes me laugh again – just when I'd pigeon-holed her as weak, she surprises me by fighting! – and I pull her back by her shoulder. "But I'm not going to let you go, either."

This time she screams her lungs out, and struggles. The heat blazes through me, and I'm hard again. I might actually do a Michael Hutchence one day – but do it properly, obviously. I think it would be something I'd like.

She's stopped screaming and struggling before my brain's acknowledged that she's still because I've ignored her. I'm lucky there's no one on the beach. The Lord moves in mysterious ways.

Kilve, January 2022

Portia

The moment I realise that I am slung like a bag around Richard's neck, thinking *Liam could be dead, Liam could be dead,* is the moment that I realise what 'love 'really means. It's overwhelming. It's pure. Richard is saying things, but something's happened to me and although I am aware that he is speaking, my brain won't process the words. My brain won't process the words because what he's saying isn't important – what's important is that I find a way of helping Liam. If I'd had one of the old 90s phones that had buttons, I know I'd have been able to work out which ones to press just by the feel of it in my back pocket. But I have a new iPhone, and I've never had one before. I don't know if I can just swipe, hit somewhere near the bottom of the screen for 'emergency call 'and go from there – I've been too busy installing apps and playing with the camera. Fucking hell, I'm so shallow. Liam was right. Oh my God. What if he dies and that's how he remembers me?!

Richard has put me on the floor, so I make to run, but I'm uber aware of my heeled boots, and I hesitate, and he grabs me, and I am looking back across the beach, and I can see the dark shape of Liam, prone on the cold stones. The red around him stands out against the neutral pallet of the shingle beach. I've been screaming, but Richard has gone … blank. It's like he's not here. I stop screaming because there's no one else on the beach, and it isn't making any difference, and then he asks me about going on holiday to the Isle of Wight. I think he is insane. I glance back at Liam, and it's like his blood is screaming at me to do something.

I want to know – desperately need to know – what Richard is thinking, but I can't bring myself to speak. Also, I'm terrified of whatever it is that's on his mind. We are in the car, in silence, and he seems very far away. I wonder if he should be driving, and nearly laugh at that thought, because he's probably planning to rape me and kill me – it's nothing he hasn't done before – and I think I'd rather die in a car crash. And then I remember that Liam is dying *right now*. With a glance at Richard to check that he is still lost in his sick thoughts, I reach my left hand behind me and try to get my phone out of my jeans pocket. If I keep it down by my thigh, I might be able to dial 999 without him noticing, and then strike up a conversation for them to overhear –

"Put your phone away, Portia."

That's that then. This man will kill me.

Journey from Kilve to Eskwich, January 2022

Richard
I enjoy driving. It's something I can do on autopilot, while my brain goes off and calibrates everything for me. Portia froze up again when I put her in the car, so the journey from Kilve back to my flat is peaceful. The scenery is beautiful, and there's not much traffic on the roads. Perfect. I can hear myself think. I can feel that things are finally beginning to happen for me. Every shitty little thing I've been through has had its purpose … ha! The Lord moves in mysterious ways!

One of my earliest memories is of being at school, drawing a dinosaur. A Tyrannosaurus Rex, to be exact. Every little boy's favourite dinosaur. I saw, through the miraculous workings of social media, a post on Facebook the other day. Someone I'd never met was quoting someone else, who'd they'd never met, who had posted something on Twitter that said *the worst thing about being an adult is that people stop asking what your favourite dinosaur is. It s like they don t even care.* I have no idea how Facebook's algorithms work in conjunction with those of other social media platforms, but it gave me the feeling that the Universe had touched me in some way. Universe with a capital 'U', out of respect to a hippy-dippy girl I once knew. Kayleigh. My nan would have said *the Lord moves in mysterious ways.* They would have hated each other for it, which is ironic, because the sentiment is the same. Anyway, I digress.

I must have been about six or seven years old when I was drawing that dinosaur. The whole class was drawing dinosaurs. We were doing a project that lasted many joyful weeks and had a profound effect on the course of my life. I remember being engrossed. When I'd finished, I thought it was the best thing I had ever done. I wanted to colour it in. We had pencil crayons that day, which I thought was the next best thing to paint. I chose a red and a green, and I blended them to try to show how the light was hitting my Tyrannosaurus Rex, and where he was hottest. I figured that – as with humans – the area around his mouth and eyes and throat would be full of blood vessels. I put a lot of thought into it, took my time, and produced a picture that, to my mind, was beautiful and realistic.

I dutifully raised my hand when the teacher asked who had finished their drawing. Mrs Hill came over and had a look. She laughed. Then she took the green pencil crayon and, pressing really hard, coloured over the bottom half of my dinosaur. Then she took the red one and coloured over the head. *Now that s better,* she said, *I think we re going to have to work on your colouring, aren t we, Richard?!*

I picked up the coloured pencils from where she'd dropped them on the table and stabbed them through the back of her hand.

But only in my mind's eye.

Bitches have always had it in for me. They can't be trusted. And I'm not a chicken-shit little school-boy anymore.

"Put your phone away, Portia."

Portia

His voice is ice-cold. *He* is ice-cold. I think of the properties of ice. Cold, hard, capable of cutting you, killing you, but also of preserving things. And breakable, like 'skating on thin ice'. And it's water, so given different conditions, it can metamorphosise. Thinking of this calms me, and, eventually, the shock wears off and I stop crying. Salt water. Salt water reminds me of that saying. Something like, *salt water is the cure for everything, be it sweat, tears, or the sea.* Well, I've been to the seaside, I've cried, so maybe it's a case of 'third time lucky': I need to sweat. Which means working out how to get out of this, and how to get help for Liam. I push down the memory of his blood spreading over the beige and grey rocks, trickling into rock pools. I can't do anything about that right now, and getting upset will only make things worse. Even though ice-man seems preoccupied, I know he's watching me. It's creepy. He's weird. *That's all he is, Porche, a fucking weirdo.* This thought makes me smile. I wait until the atmosphere has returned to its original state. Then I say, as nonchalantly as I'm able,

"Well, this is boring. Can't you at least put some music on or something?"

"Oh, hello!" he says, spritely. There: I've warmed him up and he's changed form. He turns to face me, briefly, and his face has opened up into this, frankly, gorgeous smile. "You can put that C- … ugh … blue memory stick in if you like," he says.

"You were going to say 'CD', weren't you?" I tease. "No wonder you're into dinosaurs – you bloody *are* one!"

Richard freezes again, and with it comes the fear that I've gone too far, but it's only momentarily. He laughs.

"Do you know, Liam's mum said something like that to me once," he says, conversationally. "When she was younger than you, actually. A long time before she was murdered."

With 'murdered', he looks at me again, and smiles malignantly. I take a subtle deep breath. *Keep yourself together, Porche!*

There are lots of flash drives in the cup-holder bit, below the gear stick, but the blue one is actually in the wrinkled leather around the gear stick. He must use it a lot. When I press the button to switch the stereo on, Radio Four comes up.

"Radio Four?!" The words are out of my mouth before I've thought about it. Shit.

"Yes. You should listen to it from time to time," Richard states, his eyes fixed on the meandering road ahead, "you might learn something." A pause. "Also, I like the shipping forecast. Keeps one grounded, as it were. Ironically."

Keep calm, Porche.

I insert the memory stick into the USB point and touch the screen on the dashboard.

"What's this? It sounds like Noel Gallagher."

"That's because it is Noel Gallagher. Noel Gallagher's High-Flying Birds, to be exact. If you don't like it, put the other stick in."

I look at the words coming up on the infotainment screen on his dashboard. Noel Gallagher's High-Flying Birds. The track is called *Dead in the Water*. Involuntarily, I gasp. Liam. I rip the flash drive out of the USB, grab another, and shove it in.

Faithless '*Insomnia* fills the car. Without taking his eyes from the road, Richard puts it on repeat. That's cool with me – it's a classic.

I'm trying to keep track of my surroundings. Richard is driving back a different route to the way Liam drove in. I presume we're going back, because the signs for Minehead have disappeared, although where 'back 'is to Richard, I don't know. We seem to be skirting Exmoor, and we've crossed the Devon/Somerset border so many times I wonder if he's lost – but Richard doesn't seem like the sort of person who gets lost.

It's dimpsy now, and the woods we're driving through are starting to look menacing. After a bit, Richard flips the headlights on. Actually, his car's so fancy and new that they probably switched themselves on. I gasp again and actually jump in my seat when they're reflected in the eye of a monster. Richard laughs, and the deer spins, lurching back from the road, where it's consumed by the darkness of the trees.

The volume of the music renders conversation impossible, and I try not to let my mind wander. I try to keep track of the names of villages we pass through, try to remember what time it was when Liam and I arrived at Kilve, and what the carpark had looked like, what the beach had looked like. We weren't far from a low cliff, and there was a stream that came from nowhere and ran straight over the stones to the sea. It was more like a perpetual spillage than a stream. It hadn't looked normal. But then nor had the beach itself. If I was going to make a movie set on a different planet, I'd shoot it at Kilve. It was unearthly. I didn't like it.

I have no idea how long we've been driving. It's so hard to keep track of time. Not being able to use my phone has made me realise how much I use my phone. And how much I rely on it. It's been so long that the music feels like some kind of sensory deprivation torture. Richard's turned to ice again. His face is set like he's a plastic model of himself. Fear is taking hold of me again.

I have never been so relieved to see the sign for Bampton. Not even after the time me and my best mate, Chelsea, snuck out of our parents 'houses and tried to walk to the Fair. If I could just get my seatbelt off and open the door, I could throw myself out of the car when we go past the Horseshoe Inn, and just start screaming. And that would be that. It's a simple thing to do. I can do this. I have to do this. My right hand hovers over the red button on the seatbelt - the road straightens out - I can see people walking - one fluid movement, press, open, roll – last minute, left hand, or he'll see – wait – NOW!

"You know your name means 'pig', don't you?"

Seatbelt alarm is dinging – left hand slips on the handle – head smashes against the window - thrown myself to the left but I'm stuck in the car – roll again -

"The child-lock is on, Portia. Now, answer me. I was thinking of you as being dog-like, but really, you're a pig. Did you know that your name means 'pig'?"

I'm disoriented. My head is banging. My left hand pulls and pulls at the doorhandle, but it won't budge. We're through Bampton, back in the woods. Richard swerves the car off the road and we screech into a layby. He turns the car off.

"PORTIA!" He's in my face, screaming at me. "ANSWER THE FUCKING QUESTION!"

This time I can't stop the tears. I cry loudly, sobs wracking my body, nose running, saliva down my chin. I beat my thighs with my fists, rocking back and forth in my seat, think about smashing my forehead into the dashboard – Richard is out of his seat and on top of me, pinning my wrists to the headrest with one hand, the other round my throat so I can't headbutt him - squashing me so I can't breathe – vice-like hand pushing on my windpipe –

"You're a pig in a farrowing crate, Portia! There's nothing you can do! Calm the fuck down!"

I struggle harder, spit in his face – he grins, lunges at me – tongue in my mouth, I bite down – something crunches - taste metal – a howl " –FUCKING BITCH!" – he spits red at me, raises his fist -

Eskwich, January 2022

Richard

I swing the car off Bridge Road and into my driveway. I cut the engine, throw the door open, haul myself out, and spit blood as I yank the double doors to the courtyard shut.

Fucking bitch! Portia's still out cold in the passenger seat, so I slam the open door closed, lock the car and head upstairs. I'd just got the smell of blood out of this bathroom, and now it's dripping on the floor again, mixed with saliva, and it's all I can taste.

I glare into the bathroom mirror and open my mouth. Bitch! She's bitten onto the fluorescent dice on my tongue piercing! Forced the fucking thing into my tongue! It's carnage in there! Its corners were sharp anyway, used to scratch the roof of my mouth to hell but I kind of liked that. I tease the yellow dice out of my tongue, unscrew it, take the whole bar out, and drop it onto the side of the sink. She's torn the hole! This is going to get infected! I spit pink into the basin, then swig from the Listerine bottle. It stings like fuck, but I keep swilling it round my mouth while I count to sixty in my head. Another spit into the sink. The pain is worse now the liquid's out. I rinse out the basin and mop the floor with some loo roll. Then, after slamming the bathroom door, I storm into the living room, grab a bottle of Smirnoff and neck it until I don't hurt anymore. Time to get the pig-dog out of the car.

I have to sling her over my shoulder again, a carcass in an abattoir. Once she's upstairs, I lay her carefully on my bed, and wonder what the odds are of me getting her jeans off without her waking up. She's a pretty girl, and spontaneously feisty, too. Reminds me a bit of Kayleigh, but with better hair. I smooth her long, straight locks and fan them out onto my crisp, white sheets. I see why Liam likes her. I take a Dettol wipe out of the packet I keep next to the bed (a hangover from my dead ex) and wipe the dirt and blood off her face and hands. I'd have had to keep her here for a few days even if I hadn't been planning to, because the bruises are coming up already. I trace the contours of her body, finally brushing her lips with my thumb. I kiss her lips, take her hand in mine, and lie down next to her. Sleep.

Liam

Me and Dad are standing outside Grumfer's place. We've cleared it and cleaned it, and Dad's just locked the front door for the last time. We look from the cluttered window of the bike shop to the grotty net curtains of what used to be Grumfer's front room window, next door. Dad asked me back along if I wanted the place. He said I could rent it, and we'd make it work. He was always going to take over the bike shop. I think he'd known that since he was a little boy. I think he thought I might forget about university; that Grumfer's deterioration might compel me to stay around my family, my roots. I think he thought we could run the bike shop together, me living next door, pass the business and the house down through the generations; to be honest, part of me got caught up in the romance of it all, too, but I couldn't. I couldn't envision waking up every morning, opening my curtains and looking out at the funeral directors. And it wasn't just the office-y part of the business – it was the place where people went to see their loved ones 'sleeping'; the place where the embalmer injected formaldehyde into dead bodies, plugged their butts, forced lifeless limbs into the last clothes they'd ever wear, covered up wounds with make-up … No, I couldn't have lived there even if it hadn't been Grumfer's place. It would have been like living with ghosts, and worse, because Grumfer wasn't even dead. He was in a fucking care home. He was in a fucking care home because me and Dad were incapable of looking after an old man who was here one minute, not knowing who I was the next; boiling spuds for his tea in the kettle; banging on about when his mum and dad used to take him on holiday to the Isle of Wight; accidentally burning down whole terraces. Also, I love dinosaurs. Prehistory. And I can't wait to be free from this shithole of a town. Life is for the living. God, that isn't a million miles away from fucking *YOLO*.

We just stand there, in the middle of the road, until Dad says, "Right. Do you want to nip in The Riverboat for a quick a pint before I drop the keys up to the estate agent?"

Richard

I'm a survivor – my instincts are sharp, and I'm hyperaware. My eyes spring open. Quiet. Portia's hand is still firmly within my grasp. I turn my head slowly to the right, to look at her. Her lids are flicking and she's wincing. I watch. She jolts awake. Sitting bolt upright, I wait while she takes in her surroundings and realises her left hand is captive. She gasps. She turns. She looks at me in horror, so I smile at her.

"Wakey, wakey, Sleeping Beauty!" I say, still smiling. She tries to pull her hand free, and eventually I let her. She scrambles to the other side of the bed, still looking at me as if I'm Freddy Kruger, or something. I sit up, slowly, and stretch while she checks herself out. *Fully clothed? Check. Am I hurt? Yes, but it s only my head. Am I bleeding? I have been. Where s my phone? Still in my back pocket. I haven t been raped. Where am I?*

"You're at my house, Portia. This is my bedroom. If you come out into the front room, I'll get you a coffee and something to eat, and we can talk about things, but feel free to use the bathroom and clean yourself up. You can use my mouthwash, is you like." My voice sounds funny. My throat is sore. *Where s the bathroom?* "It's just along the hall." I pause and wait for her to smile. She doesn't. "Relax, Portia. It'll be alright," I say gently, reaching over to touch her hand. In spite of herself, she smiles. Stockholm Syndrome. She gets off the bed and walks down the hall, her heeled boots clicking on the floorboards. She reaches the bathroom door, which is shut. I remember, I slammed it earlier. She looks at me. *Is this the bathroom door?* I slammed it earlier because she tore my tongue and ruined my favourite tongue stud. That's why I'm lisping. "Yes, that's the door to the bathroom." I pause. She opens the door, places one foot inside, and shyly smiles back at me.

Thank you. Bitch.

"I'd use the shower, though, instead of the bath. Someone died in there."

Eskwich, 2021

Liam

When I found out I'd got my place at Liverpool Uni, Dad had told me to break up with Portia. That was the first thing he'd said. Not, *Congratulations! Let s go for a pint!* He just made that noise that people do when they're taking the piss out of a mechanic or a plumber or something, like, *I can fix it, but it ll cost ya,* and then he said, *well, that s the end of you and Portia, then. Shame, that – she s a nice girl.* To be fair, after he'd said that, he'd slapped me on the back and said, *Well done though, kiddo. That s your ticket out.* And *your grumfer would ve been proud,* which had almost made me cry.

I don't think he'll ever tell me the whole story about what happened between him and Mum, but I get the impression that he thinks you're better off staying well out of relationships. Or, if you have to be in one, you shouldn't get too attached. He's definitely never had a girlfriend since, and I don't think that's just because he's still in love with Mum or anything. He hardly ever goes out. He just works and then comes home and sits in front of the telly drinking cider until it's time to go to bed. I wouldn't say he's depressed or anything, either. It's more like he's exhausted, but he daren't stop. It's like if he stops working, he'll start thinking, and he doesn't want to.

There are no pictures of Mum in the house – that I know of - except for the one he's got in the front of his phone case, and the one he gave me that I keep in my room. It's a picture of me and her that my nan took when I was a baby. It's a happy photo. I'm on Mum's lap in the front room of the old flat she and Dad used to rent in Thomas Street. We're on the sofa. She's holding a yoghurt up for me, and I've obviously just dunked both my hands in it and started clapping. We're both laughing. Dad put it in a frame for me.

Every year on the day before the summer solstice, Dad and I go up along the canal, picking wildflowers, and then he drives us up to Stonehenge. He told me he was really sneaky, and when him and my nan had picked up Mum's ashes, they'd gone down The Riverboat for a drink. Partly to toast Mum, partly to deal with the shock, and partly because they just didn't know what to do with each other. Anyway, after half a bottle of merlot, Nan had gone to the loo. Dad said he'd opened the casket, grabbed a handful of ashes, and put them in one of those money bags you get from the bank. He'd said some flakes fell on the floor and over the seat, but Mum wouldn't have minded because she spent half her life in the pub anyway. He'd said she would have thought it was funny.

And then he'd gone to Stonehenge, thinking you could just walk up to the stones and sit on them or something, with the grand plan of sprinkling her ashes there. She'd been a right fucking hippy, he'd said, and a piece of her heart had always been at Stonehenge – although he didn't know if she'd ever gone there - so he'd thought he'd put a bit of her body there, too. But when he got there, he'd found it was all cordoned off, and the only way you could get near the stones was to do a tour. There were loads of tourists there, so he'd put the earphones on with the rest of them and then gone off for a virtually-guided-tour. You couldn't really stop anywhere, so he said he'd kind of leaked Mum out as he'd gone round, pouring little bits as far inside the barrier as he was able. He said that at least this way she gets to be there for the summer solstice every year, and party with the druids and that.

And now we go up the day before the solstice, so we don't have to deal with the hippies, dribble our flowery offering around, have a bit of a laugh and then go for a McDonald's.

But anyway, Dad had been cross when I'd told him me and Portia were going to try to make a go of it. He'd said I was wasting my time, and that we'd only end up cheating on each other and getting heartbroken. That we should take a leaf out of Chris Martin and Gwyneth Paltrow's book and make a 'conscious uncoupling'. I'd told him to fuck off. Portia and I love each other. And we'd done it, as well. There was only a problem when Covid hit.

I've often thought it about my dad – although I know it's each to their own – but they say being on your own a lot drives you mad. You go into your own head and get lost there. I didn't think either Portia or me would have a problem with a lockdown – I was up at uni with my mates, which was a hell of a lot better bubble to be in than watching Netflix constantly with my dad; she had her family. I know they'd closed the college, but everyone does all their shit online nowadays anyway, so it's not like she wouldn't see her mates. And we could Zoom and do FaceTime and that. I didn't think it would be too bad. And anyway, it wouldn't be for long.

And it was okay at the start. Because she couldn't work in New Look anymore, she started doing online stuff with The Body Shop. Selling make-up and that, trialling it online, making videos and shit. Then when she got an order, she'd post it off to whoever, and the money came in by PayPal. So, she was earning, and it looked like she was making a shed load from it. She said she could pay for me to come down on the train - first class! She had a focus. I kind of got into the habit of checking her out on Instagram to see what she was doing. To be fair, she was good at her job. She always wore make-up and she always knew how to do it properly, like they do on TV and that, not like the girls at school used to do it - slapping it on with their fingers and blending it in as best they could. Portia had a load of brushes and contraptions. It used to take her fucking ages, but once she'd done it, she looked beautiful, like model, or something.

She used to phone me and say how much work she was

getting done now she couldn't go out. The internet was basically the only tool she needed for research, so she was good. She was looking at unis, trying to come up to Liverpool with me and do History, but then I said I was going to do my Masters in Palaeontology at Manchester, so she said she'd come up with me, do her first degree there, and we could share a flat. It sounded like a plan to me, but Dad went mental.

And then I started really enjoying being in Liverpool. No Dad, people who were actually *alive* - moving about; the place had an energy that just doesn't exist in Devon. And my housemates were awesome. It was hilarious, even when Covid hit, and we were captive. We did our courses online. We couldn't get out in the field, but we could watch a load of videos and read a load of stuff. We made do, like everyone else did. And we took it in turns to run down to Food Booze News for alcohol. To be fair, we were wasted a lot of the time, and my mate, Jay took up 'jogging 'with his dealer, so we were never short of skunk, either.

One Friday night me and Jay were sat on the corner-sofa, watching shit on telly, smoking weed and flicking through our phones. I happened to glance up, saw him smiling his secret smile, and his thumbs were a blur, he was typing so fast.

"So, who are you texting every ten seconds, then?!" I teased.

"Ah, mate, I think I'm in love, you know?!"

"Are you fuck!" I said. "Is she real this time?"

"What do you mean?"

"Well, Skylar said the last bird you were seeing turned out to be a fat Brummie perv!" I dissolved into laugher.

"Fuck off, man!" he said, chucking a handful of chips at me.

I picked them up off the floor and stuffed them into my mouth. "Two second rule," I said, flicking a smile at him. "So, who is she then?"

I got off the sofa, walked round, and leaned over the back of the bit he was sitting on, so I could see his phone. I couldn't believe my eyes.

"Fit, isn't she?" Jay said.

I just stood there with my mouth open, not knowing what to say. Jay was on Instagram. He was looking at a photo of Portia. One that I'd never seen. She was kneeling on a picnic blanket, wearing the bottom half of a leopard print bikini, holding a glass of Champagne or something, legs splayed, kind of leaning forward, looking that look. She looked like a model. She looked like a porn star, or something.

"Who the fuck is that?" I said.

"Some bird called Porche," Jay replied. "You should follow her. You've got to pay for it, but fuck me is it worth it?!"

"What do you mean, pay for it?"

"Dude, she's on OnlyFans! You don't get to see shit like this on her normal profile!"

"OnlyFans?"

Jay swung round on the sofa to face me, nearly knocking me out. He was laughing, this incredulous smile spread over his face. "Seriously, Lee, you're not telling me you've never heard of OnlyFans?!

"Oh my God! This is brilliant! Sit down, boy, get your pen out and take some notes, because I am about to educate you!"

So that was why she was so flush. Bitch. My dad had been right. She'd be down 'Tesco's Pillars 'with the rest of the prossies next. I felt like calling her and giving her shit down the phone. I felt like signing up and seeing what else she was posting. But what I actually did was, nothing.

Except shag Atlantis.

Portia

I'd use the shower though, instead of the bath. Someone died in there.'

My blood freezes, again, even though I know he said it with the express purpose of freaking me out. Mind games.

I close the bathroom door behind me and slip a bit on the floor, nearly hitting my head on the sink. I sit there in the middle of the room, letting the tears fall, trying not to look at the bath. I look at the bath. It's clean – like *uber* clean – but I can clearly see pink stains in the grouting. I wonder about who had died there, and I wonder if Richard had had anything to do with it. He's going to kill me if I don't do something. I know he is. I have to calm down. I quickly scan the room for a means of escape. There's a tiny window with that thick, streaked glass that lets the light in but you can't see through it. I stand on the toilet seat, craning my neck out of the bit at the top that opens. There's no way on God's green earth I'm going to get out of that, and even if by some miracle I made it, I'm like two storeys up. I'd be smashed to pieces on Bridge Road, and then some fucking boy-racer would come and run me over for good measure.

"Knock, knock …" Richard is just outside the door. I can almost feel the heat of his breath coming through the panelled wood. My head whips round, and before I can even think about stealthily climbing down from the loo seat, he's in the bathroom, chuckling at me.

"Oh, Portia. I admire your tenacity, but just get yourself clean and comfortable. Come on! If I'd wanted to rape you, I'd have had a go while you were spark-o, and if I'd wanted to kill you, I would have done it already! Probably." I get off the toilet seat and stand in front of him, glaring. He stands there, grinning back at me.

"Well, are you going to fuck off, then, or what?!"

He laughs. "Actually, Portia, I was hoping to watch, but

if you need your privacy, I'll step outside for a bit." He closes the door, too gently, and I wait a bit before I strip off and get in the shower - I wouldn't put it past him to pop his head back round the door. He doesn't.

As soon as I stop the water, I realise I'll have to put on my old clothes. They'd been clean on this morning, but just the thought of putting them back on makes me feel sick. I needn't have worried, though: a pile of clothes has appeared on the side of the bath. Fucking bastard. But I put them on.

Now I feel more like myself, I'm hungry, so I wander into the front room. Richard is leaning out of one of the big sash windows, smoking. I think about running over and slamming it down on him. It'd break his spine, surely. I think about throwing my phone to shatter the glass, and I imagine it slicing down through him, impaling him to the windowsill like in that scene at the end of *Ghost*, when the evil guy in the suit finally gets his Karma. Actually, where *is* my phone?

"I'll put the kettle on when I've finished my fag," Richard says. This guy is like a robot, or like Jack Reacher, or something. He also enjoys head-fucking people, and I need to remember that.

"Where's my phone?"

"Portia!" he teases, "Don't be so aggressive!" He nods to the low coffee table. "I'll be honest," he says, "I did have a go at guessing your password, but it seems you're cleverer than I thought."

I swipe the phone up off the table. I don't know whether to believe him or not, but turning it over and over in my hand isn't going to help. His fingerprints will be on it anyway, because he picked it up to move it. But, really, as long as he hasn't been through my Insta account, I don't care. It always makes me laugh when people are so precious about their privacy. The amount of mates I've got who've deleted their Facebook accounts because they're worried about someone stealing their identity. I mean, how fucking arrogant, or self-obsessed or whatever it is – who on earth is going to give a fuck about what you had for tea or where you've been, or scrolling through photos of you pissed on dancefloors and that? Get over yourself! Most of them are in their overdrafts or have maxed out their credit cards - it's not like they've got any cash to steal! Having said that, I really don't like the idea of Richard looking at my OnlyFans page. But then he's just seen me naked in the shower. I wonder how long he was there. And none of it makes any sense anyway – my body is just a body. It's not like it's my soul. And it's making me money. The whole thing is weird.

I get really pissed off with all the airbrushing and shit, and false eyelashes and boob jobs. I made this TikTok video the other day. I stood up straight, pulled in my tummy and did a little dance, and then I let my tummy go, so I had a little muffin top. Then I leaned over, right in front of the camera, and squidged my belly will both my hands. Just to show that the angle a photo is taken at makes all the difference, and that what you see is never the whole story. All these girls, slicing themselves to bits, starving themselves, hating themselves, having surgery they don't need, and Botox and that. You can't change the fact that you are alive. I remember that Dr Who episode, with a race of aliens or people in the future or whatever, this woman had turned herself into a piece of skin stretched over an easel, with a pair of eyes and a mouth, and she thought she'd achieved perfection, but she couldn't walk, she had no hands, she couldn't do anything, and someone had to be next to her the whole time misting her with water so she didn't dry out. But she thought she was perfect.

It drives me to despair when I'm not laughing about it: we're supposed to be so enlightened and that now, and it's worse than it ever was; the racism, the body issues, the climate change and the planet and consumerism. It's all such a load of bollocks. We're all just here, and we don't know why – not for certain; not with proof – so why don't we just accept that we're here, survive in the best way we can, and try to enjoy it? I mean, what else have we got? It's a cliché, but it's true: *you only live once.*

I find myself standing next to Richard, pulling a Marlboro out of the packet he's offered me. I lean my head out of the window, and watch all the people flocking down to the pub. The town hall clock chimes eight. Liam could be dead, taken up by the tide, bobbing either up to Bristol, or into the Irish Sea. But I don't think that's true. My gut's saying he's stronger than that. All I can do is stay sharp and bide my time.

Liam

Dragging myself over these rocks is a shite sight easier than walking over them. The thought makes me laugh. I'll have to tell Porche that when I see her again, and this keeps me going. I imagine her cracking up, punching me on the arm because she knows I could have died. I am fucking cold. It's numbed me, though, so I can pull myself through the rock pools. I just have to keep my head up, out of the water. It's banging still. On autopilot, I reach up my good arm to check if the bleeding has stopped, but my fingers don't feel anything, and I can't see a thing. I might be dying. I might be hypothermic. It must be adrenaline that's keeping me going, and I need to get as far away from the sea, as near as I can to civilisation before it wears off. I could die. Porche knows I could have died. So why hasn't she phoned an ambulance? Why has no one come looking for me? Where's the *choppa choppa* of the helicopter thing … the air-ambulance? The first thing I did was feel around me for my phone, because it wasn't in my pocket, but I couldn't find it. It could have fallen out at any time. Unless Richard took it, or Porche had it. We argued in the car – again – on the way out here, about OnlyFans. She called me misogynistic! How on earth can she say that, when all I'm trying to do is stop her exploiting herself online? The thought of Jay wanking over her is bad enough, but all those creepy nonces on the internet?! I'm moving faster now; outrage is forcing me forwards. She was angry, but she wouldn't have left me here to die. What if Richard did the same to her, and she was out cold and couldn't hear me calling for her?! What if I've left her to drown?! Panic rises. All I can do is keep going, keep going, and get to a phone and call the police. I'm crying. My hands are splashing water. I'm more vertical. I'm at the stream! I'm nearly at the cliff! My momentary joy freezes over – Richard wouldn't have left Portia. He wouldn't have left her, because he would have wanted to fuck her. That's what he does. He raped my mum, and now he's raping my girlfriend! I haul myself to my feet, and vertigo hits. I throw up. I am numb, but I can tell that the ground beneath my feet is soft – it sounds hollow. We'd walked through a field. We'd taken a dirt path off to the right. Before that, there'd been a lane, full of puddles. A long dirt track through trees. Then the carpark. But the carpark had been in two lengthy sections, separated by a picnic area – I'd pulled over and parked as soon as I'd seen the parking metre. We'd had no change, and I couldn't get a phone signal to go on the RingGo app, so we hadn't paid. I bet I've been clamped. And then, the main road and the shop literally on the corner …? Hope pushes me on. I'm lurching like a drunk, grabbing at bits of hedge. No. Before the carparks was about a mile of winding road. Portia thought we'd gone the wrong way. Past a derelict church. Had we turned off to the right? I remember driving down a steep hill. Winding, always winding. Fucking country lanes! Winding and narrow. And interminably long. I haven't got a hope in hell. I stumble into a pothole, or a rabbit hole – a hole. Fall on my knees. Cry harder. Curl up on my side. Richard has Portia. He'll torture her and then he'll kill her, and I can't do a fucking thing about it. The tears have stopped. I have no idea where I am or how to get to where I need to be. Can't do anything without light. Have to wait here till morning. Tired. Really tired. But not cold anymore. And I've stopped shaking.

Eskwich, January 2022

Richard

Well, this is nice! The beautiful Portia and I, spending Saturday night drinking vodka and flat lemonade in companionable silence. We're sitting side by side, our backs up against the radiator under my favourite window – the one I smoke out of. I have the sash pulled up so we can hear the scum of Eskwich making their way to their favourite drains. The Riverboat is the place most of them go to, by virtue of it being a 'spoons now. Big place, cheap beer. The Stars has its regulars and they've got a band on tonight – they're the only place in town that do live music now; the only place with a jukebox, actually – which will either mean they get their highest or lowest takings of the month. Life's a gamble, isn't it?

I'd offered Portia a straight, out of politeness – after all, she has her vape – but we've ended up chain smoking the whole packet. I need to pop to the corner shop to get some more, but I don't really want to leave her here on her own. I ought to get us something to eat, too. I don't want her passing out on me. Not from lack of food, anyway. Dilemma.

My mind is made up when I try to pour us another drink each, and nothing comes out of the vodka bottle. It's a shame Dominos don't do alcohol. They do Coke, though, which is better than flat lemonade. Fuck it. I'll order a pizza and nip out for a nice bottle of wine. I wonder if Jerry's do Champagne.

"Give me your phone, Portia." The vodka has taken the edge off the pain of my ruined tongue but talking is a bit of an effort and my voice sounds wrong.

"Why?" She's slurring a bit. Her face is flaccid, rubbery.

"Because I'm going out."

"Can I come?" She giggles, flopping onto her elbows, grinning like the Cheshire Cat.

"Ordinarily, that would be delightful, Portia. Unfortunately for you, you are my hostage, so, no. No, you can't come with me. Rest assured, I won't be gone long, but I don't want you making any silly phone calls in my absence."

At first, she smiles, but then her expression becomes harsh. I wonder how drunk she actually is. "Liam could be dead, you know."

"I know." I grab my leather jacket off the banister and pull it on. Nice and warm.

"But then you'll be a murderer, won't you? Didn't you go to prison once?"

How does she know that? I thought Liam didn't talk about me. Maybe he really does like this girl. Interesting.

"If you go back in, the only way you'll come out, is in a box," she says. "I thought you just got tenure. I thought you wanted to discover a dinosaur. What's the point of keeping me here if Liam is dead? Unless you're going to kill me, too. I could shout out of the window, you know. I could have done it by now if I'd wanted to. And anyway, Liam could help you. Be your assistant or something. He always says it's best to dig in a team so you can cover more ground more quickly and help each other with tricky bits. And big fossils must be heavy -"

"Give me your phone, Portia."

Her face crumbles.

"I lied, by the way. I did work out your password." I gently take the phone from her hand, and stare at her until the first fresh tears start to fall. I unlock the phone, pressing the letters Y O L O, and make a call, staring into her lovely eyes while I speak.

"The coastguard, I think. And an ambulance."

I speak as quickly as I can, hang up, take the sim card out, take both it and the handset to my work bench, and smash them with my hammer.

Pulling my phone from my back pocket, I ask her, "Meat

Feast okay with you?”

Portia

Richard's a psycho. I think there's something really wrong with him. He's called for help for Liam. I hope against hope that it's not too late. He's smashed my phone. And now he's just 'nipped out 'for another bottle of vodka. I am in the flat alone. I could try to climb out of one of the big windows and creep down the wall, but I'm not Count Dracula. I could lean out of the window and shout to someone, but I feel pretty pissed now, and everyone walking by seems to be wasted, too. That or deeply involved in a heart-to-heart, or an argument. I find myself listening. No one seems to have any shame – you can hear everything! 'Jess 'has shagged 'Luke 'behind her best mate's back, and she's trying to fob her off with the excuse that they were both pissed up and it didn't mean anything. It was 'Bradley 'who set fire to the car at the bottom of Thomas Street, because 'Stuart 'didn't pay up on time. I don't want to think about Stuart, so I immerse myself in another conversation, one between two young mums. Apparently, there's a new playgroup started up in Moorhayes Community Centre, that does 'proper ' coffee, and Marks and Spencer's biscuits … I've spent too long listening out of the window – I could be looking round the flat.

Minimal furniture, wooden floors, white walls, no pictures. Like, no photos, or anything. It's spectacularly clean. There's a massive flat-screen TV on the far wall of the living room – the other side's a banister and then the stairs to the front door. The kitchen is just off this room. Almost open plan. The bathroom. No frills, modern, again, all white. I bet if he used Cillit Bang, he could get the blood out of the grouting. A giggle escapes me, because I can't believe I'm thinking like this! I must be in shock, or something. And I'm pissed. Going back to the kitchen, I open all the cupboards until I find a glass, and then down

about a pint of water. I need to stay sharp. The bedroom –
guess what. All white. Except in here there's an ornament
of one of those flying dinosaurs. What is it? The one that
starts with the silent 'p'. Pterodactyl, or something? It's
pretty big – about the size of a cat – in turquoisey colours.
I can't believe that Richard's got tenure, and endgame for
him is discovering a dinosaur. I bet it's only so he can name
it after himself. I mean, he could actually do something
useful like try to find the meteor that killed them all off –
proof that that's what happened, or something. That's what
Liam wants to do. Richard's a narcissist. And that's my way
out of this.

There's a closed door at the end of the hall, and when I
push it, I expect it to be locked. It isn't, and relief rushes
through me. I just got this sudden foreboding - like I was
entering Bluebeard's secret cave, or whatever it was he had
- but if it isn't locked, it isn't secret. And if it hadn't been
locked when we got here, but he'd wanted it locked,
Richard could have sorted everything out while I was
sleeping. Sleeping?! I'd been unconscious because he'd
knocked me out! I try to remember the car journey; what
I'd said that had made him hit me. I fail.

As there's no natural light in the room, I trace the wall
with my hand to find a light switch, and when I click it on,
the room erupts into light, and I have to squint. It's like a
bloody supermarket in here!

A massive wood-topped table with industrial red legs
takes up most of the room. The walls are covered with
annotated maps, diagrams of skeletons of dinosaurs and
other animals, and hanging along one wall are tools, like
knives and brushes, hammers and chisels, and loads of
string. They must be what you use on archaeological digs.
There's a big black holdall dumped in the middle of the
table. It's packed so full the fabric's stretched tight over
lumps, and the zip looks like it's straining. Some kind of
morbid curiosity is compelling me to open it to see what's

inside, and my hand is on the zip when I notice the seagull in the corner.

Ugh! A stuffed seagull in a glass display case, standing on one of those spindly, dark wooden Victorian flower tables. I almost urge! Its beady yellow eyes are glaring at me. It looks furious! Taxidermy has always freaked me out. Not just the look of the – what are they? - Ornaments? Pieces? and the process by which they came to be stuffed, but that someone actually went out and killed the animal and brought it home, and then delicately … ugh! What do you do with the inners?! How do you stop it rotting? Formaldehyde, I suppose. I gasp, and a load of bile fills my mouth – maybe that's why there's blood in the grouting! Gross, but I guess it's better than the thought of Richard murdering someone in his bathroom! No, he's a weirdo – he would have picked it up in an antique shop or something. Clinging onto this thought, I turn my back on the seagull and head out of the room. And that's when I notice the other set of tools.

"Ah, I see you've met Noel!" Richard's dark shape fills the doorway.

"Richard!"

"That's my name – don't wear it out!"

"Let me out, please, Richard."

"Hmm. Let you out? I don't remember letting you in."

"The door was open."

"No, the door was closed. This door is always closed."

"But it was unlocked!"

"Yes, but it was closed."

He had me there. "Let me out, please, Richard."

"Hmm. No, I don't think I will. Since you've been tenacious enough to come in here, I think you deserve the guided tour."

"No – it's fine – I'm sorry, Richard. Did you get the vodka? The pizza will be here soon." I take another step towards him, although it feels too close.

"I'm sure we'll hear the delivery person banging on the door." He takes a step closer to me, and I can feel his body heat. I retreat into the room. He advances.

"This," he begins, with a sweeping gesture of his arms, "is my work room!" He beams. He's proud of it. "My personal one, anyway. My job is more of a vocation. In my spare time I travel from place to place looking for fossils, and when I find something interesting, I'm going to bring it back here to work on." He pulls some rocks from his pocket, and places them on the workbench. "Look, these are the bits of the ammonite Liam threw at me earlier. I feel as though it's my moral duty to try to piece them back together." Richard pauses. Then smashes his fist into the table.

A small scream escapes me. The rocks jump on the table and one of them falls to the floor by my feet. On impulse, I pick it up. Richard has his hand out. I place the rock onto his palm. "Thank you," he says, quietly, "Liam really made me angry." He takes a deep breath, and I try to suppress the smirk that's threatening to burst all over my face.

Richard puts his head on one side and smiles a curious smile. "Do let me in the joke, Portia."

There's menace behind it. This guy can go from hot to cold in nanoseconds.

"Well, it's just when you said that Liam made you angry, well, the last film we watched together was *The Incredible Hulk*, and he says, 'don't make me angry', and …" I trail off.

To my surprise, he laughs. "I can see that," he says. "Brilliant scientists with a terrible secret and a hard life becomes a dangerous, almost anti-superhero. Hmm. I like that, Portia. Thank you!" He gives me a genuine smile. Even though he must be nearly sixty, there's something attractive about him. Shit, snap out of it, Porche – this guy nearly killed you. I push down thoughts of Liam. The emergency services are on it. Stressing isn't going to do me any good.

"I've been on digs or on holiday to all these places," he says, looking at the maps on the walls, "but this is the place that interests me the most. I'm sure there's a major find to be made there. Maybe we could all go together? Don't you think it would be nice to spend some time by the sea?"

I can't help myself. I find myself saying, "Seriously? You'd rather go to the Isle of Wight than to America? Liam's always talking about how he wants to find a bit of the meteor that wiped the dinosaurs out, evidence of what really happened; he's not bothered about finding a new species and naming it after his grandad, or the cat he had when he was five, or whatever, he just wants to further our understanding of our planet. He says –"

"I don't give a flying fuck what Liam says, Portia. I don't give a flying fuck about his fucking noble quest for understanding. He's twenty-three! He doesn't know *a thing* about life!"

"He does!" I spit back. "He's got more integrity in his little finger than you've got in your entire body! You're just a self-obsessed FREAK!"

Richard turns to ice. He cocks his head on one side, and smiles. It's terrifying. He holds his position and his gaze for so long that I almost scream at him to hit me, to kill me. Eventually, he speaks.

"Do you know what I find fascinating about your generation, Portia?" He phrases it like a question, but I know he doesn't want an answer.

"What I find fascinating, is that you are all so obsessed with your individuality, yet you don't understand the power this could give you.

"Your generation has grown up with the internet, and all its social media platforms. You all feel you have a right to be heard. Or, rather, that the world owes you an ear, and everyone should shut up and give you your *time to shine*. And yet, dear Liam is of the opinion that it's not the individual dinosaurs that matter; no, it's the wider workings of the *universe* that matter. (Or should that be *multiverse*?) It's not the individual creatures that live that matter, it's a fucking dead rock from outer space that's important! I mean, WHAT THE ACTUAL FUCK?!

"You still don't get it, do you?! Recycle, turn your heating down, take your bike to work instead of your car, buy strawberries from England rather than fucking Ethiopia, blah, blah, blah! It's the little things that matter the *most*! One individual Baryonyx, born with a slightly longer jaw could make or break the survival of the species! It's the cumulative effect of individuals that –"

"Yes, but it doesn't fucking matter, does it?! They were all wiped out by an asteroid! What does it matter what they *could* have become?!"

Richard smiles. He walks over to the wall with the tools and selects a small knife. He rubs the blade on his jeans, then stands so close to me that I can feel the heat of his breath when he speaks.

"So, if I slit your pretty little throat with this knife, right now, your life will not have mattered? At all? To anyone?"

He presses the blade against my skin. I have a sudden urge to swallow, but I daren't, in case the movement inadvertently cuts me.

"What will – sorry, *would* - darling Liam do if I slit your throat? Would he kill himself to ease the pain of his broken heart? Would he come after me? If he came after me, he would lose, Portia, and then where would his great scientific discovery be? How would the human race survive, not knowing for sure that the extinction of the dinosaurs was due to an asteroid? How would Liam's beloved grandfather feel as he gasps for breath in a Covid-ridden care home, not knowing the true fate of some big lizards, millions of years ago? Some people don't even believe in the dinosaurs! Did you know that? Did you know that the Flat Earth Society exists, even today? Did you know that my mother believed in God? That she was an actual practising Christian, but was still the most self-centred bitch who ever lived? Yeah, fuck all these people who are dying around the world – let's look for the bloke who ate the fucking bat! Fuck the life of fucking Dave the T-Rex who caught fire in the explosion and burnt to death, leaving his wife and children to starve while the dust cloud spread over the planet! Yeah, fuck him! Let's look for the rock that randomly tumbled out of the sky!"

Richard's eyes are wild. I shudder as bits of phlegm hit my face as he speaks, ever faster and louder. His face is in my face, the knife a now uncomfortable pressure against my throat, and I think of the rock that Liam threw, the rock with the ammonite in it, the rock that shattered on a bigger rock and made Richard do this to us.

"What about the travel restrictions?"

"WHAT?!"

"What about the travel restrictions?" My whisper is a little louder this time.

Richard stares at me like I'm mad. Or like he's mad.

"Are we allowed to go to the Isle of Wight? Aren't we all supposed to be 'staying local 'still?"

In a split second, Richard is the good-looking guy with the nice smile and the fast car and the good job again. He straightens up, steps back, and hangs the knife on its peg. He sits up against the work bench like it's a pool table in a pub.

"The travel restrictions were lifted months ago, Portia! Do you not watch the news?! The sea doesn't stop eroding the land just because there's a virus going around! Our lives don't stop ticking by. If we're healthy, we have to get on with things! Listen to all those saddos making their ways between pubs! Although it does amuse me that the point of the lockdowns were to protect the NHS because they were overrun, but now hospital workers are asserting their human rights and not getting vaccinated, so that they can spread the virus to someone who – well, someone like Liam, who's gone in for a head injury – then Liam gets Covid, or Omicron, or whatever variant we're on now, can't breathe, calls another ambulance, and lo, there's the NHS overrun again! Everything about this country is ridiculous! That 'clap for carers! 'It was like a slow clap at ourselves for being such hypocritical idiots! It comes back to what I said earlier: everyone is trying to make life work for themselves, trying to survive the best way they can. And, perhaps, have a little fun on the way." He smiles again, and I flush, in spite of myself. Richard continues. "My interest in palaeontology is vital to maintaining my mental health. And taking care of ourselves is our moral responsibility!" He regards me for a while. "I should really switch to vaping."

I almost laugh at that. Almost.

We stand in silence until he recovers himself, strides over to Noel, and pats his glass sarcophagus.

"So, yeah. Noel. Lots of people are afraid of taxidermy, but they needn't be. After all, it's the gulls that are alive that will shit on your head and steal your chips. You're quite safe with a dead one. Also, I'm just trying to find the answers like anyone else, and the best place to start is with history and biology. That which we know. In a manner of speaking. I believe you're hoping to study history at university?"

"Yes."

"Which means you are an intelligent woman, even if your password is *YOLO*! But I do agree with the sentiment. We're all just trying to make the best of things, aren't we? No one wants to waste their time?" The questions are rhetorical, so I say nothing. "I presume you've read *Frankenstein.*"

I look at the tools, the knives, the microscope, while he regards Noel. It's like he's not even here, in his brain. He's totally absorbed in his thoughts. It scares me. He seems to be having the *Frankenstein* conversation in his head. He'll kill me. I have to get out of here.

We've moved around the room, and now Richard's back is to the wall. Mine is to the door. I spin and run for it – into the front room – bang my knee on the coffee table – stumble - get to the window – can't pull it up – why won't it come up?! – panicking, pulling – hear his laughter behind me – bang on the glass – *help! Help me!* Vice-like arms around my waist. I'm being dragged away from the window, thrown onto the sofa. Richard isn't laughing anymore.

Liam

Matt Hancock keeps saying the government has thrown a 'protective ring 'around care homes. Every evening, me and Dad sit and have our tea watching the press conference, watching the red lines on the graph extend upwards at an ever-steeper gradient. Dad usually cracks a beer open when they start on the numbers of Covid-related deaths. I don't know whether he does that to cope with the numbers, to blot out the horror, or to toast the individuals. Or to deal with the fact that we are incarcerated together in our home; to take the edge off.

Much as I hated it and took the piss out of him at the time, I'm glad Dad was one of the people who started stock-piling toilet rolls, tins of beans, pasta, and cans of cider. It means we don't have to worry too much about the next available Tesco delivery slot.

Tonight, I have a beer with him. I can only do so much study online. It's hard to stay 'engaged'. It's hard to concentrate for that long on a screen. It's hard to concentrate when all I can think about is how when I went to visit Grumfer, I had to stand in the flowerbed under his window and hear his glass-muffled shouts at me to *get the hell out* of his garden or he'll *call the police*.

We'd called the home, like everyone else. They're on skeleton-staff, and no one can come in. On the late news I saw these people and their elderly relatives putting their open hands up against the windows and pressing them together. It was as near as they could get to a hug, or some comfort. It was beautiful and tragic. And I wanted to do it with my Grumfer. I missed him. I was worried about him. I felt guilty as fuck that I didn't rearrange my life and care for him in his own home. I felt guilty as fuck that I knew that even if I'd done that, I wouldn't have been able to give him the care that he needs, or cope with his emotional fallout. And on top of it all, I felt guilty as fuck that all I wanted to do was get away from this town and study things that had died millions of years ago. Guilty, but compelled. And, yeah, if he'd been in his right mind, it would have been all Grumfer ever wanted, for me to be happy. But knowing that didn't make me feel any better. So the pseudo-touching of hands would have been a gesture of solidarity. Things I couldn't say, expressed without words.

Except it didn't turn out like that, because he couldn't remember who on earth I was, and I knew that he was going to catch Covid and die because they were transferring old people from hospital without testing them. It reminded me of the Holocaust gas-chambers. I had a drink with my dad, to stop myself from going into internet chatrooms about conspiracy theories.

Richard

I throw the silly bitch onto the sofa and return to the window. It's not broken, and there's no sign of anyone on the streets below. No harm done.

I regard her, lying there, crying again. I shake my head. What a state to get in! At least now she's had a shower there's no makeup running down her face, so she doesn't look like some fucked-up clown this time. She looks like a child in the wrong clothes. She's wearing Cath's clothes – tight jeans, tight black top, green checked shirt, black socks. I wonder if she put on the knickers. I bet she did – after all, she's not to know.

"Why are you crying?" I perch on the edge of the sofa, beside her. She doesn't move. I lift up under her arms and arrange her into a comfortable sitting position. She's like a doll. Very like Cath. I wonder if I could get her to dye her hair. I stroke from the top of her head to her shoulders, embrace her.

"Why are you crying?" I ask again, when her breathing has returned to normal and she's blown her nose.

She looks at me with red, puffy eyes. Ruined beauty. "Because you scare me."

Portia leans her head into my shoulder, smiles up at me, drops her eyes. I can't believe this shit. My packet of fags is still on the coffee table. I reach for them, and then remember my own advice – I must look after myself. "Can I share your vape?"

She pulls it out of Cath's back pocket. I wonder when she put it there. I must keep an eye on her. She passes it to me.

"What do you do with it?"

She laughs. "What do you mean?"

"Well, do I have to turn it on, or something?"

More laughter. "No, Rich! It's just like smoking a fag!"

Rich.

It's not like smoking a fag. It's heavy and it's hard. And it's bloody disgusting! I waft the plume of candyfloss smoke away. "That's disgusting! What the hell is it?!"

"Vanilla custard."

"Vanilla c- ! Oh my God, I'm sticking with the Marlboros!"

We both laugh. It's nice.

"Why are you scared of me, Portia?"

She raises her eyebrows, suggesting irony, but I feel her tense up. She's silent.

"Oh. You actually want me to answer that?"

"Yes."

"Fucking hell, Richard! You hit my boyfriend and leave him for dead, you knock me out, you tell me someone died in your bathroom, you tell me you could have raped me if you'd wanted to –"

"Ah, but I didn't."

She looks at me, incredulously. "That's not the fucking point! No one normal says *I could have raped you if I'd wanted to*! It's not normal! You're not normal! You were going to cut me up and stuff me like that fucking seagull!"

She's standing now, her face in my face, angry.

"'Gull', Portia, not 'seagull'. There's no such thing as a seagull. It's just another derogatory, factually incorrect term that's wormed its way into common language. I mean, most of them live inland now, so they can pick up our leftovers. People don't think. They just let drivel pour out of their mouths unchecked. It's like this *I'm a bit OCD* phrase people keep spouting out – it's not even grammatically correct! Drives me mental!" My hand shoots out to thump the table, but I catch myself.

"What do you mean?" She sits down next to me. "*I'm* a bit OCD – I can't bear getting mud on my boots, and I have to wipe any off as soon as I see it! And with the tins of beans and that in the cupboards - I like all the labels facing the same way."

"You just said 'I'm a bit Obsessive Compulsive Disorder'. That doesn't even make sense. Do you even know what OCD is?" She stares at me. "OCD is a debilitating mental illness, not a personality quirk. My ex-girlfriend – no, fuck it – my *dead* girlfriend, Cath had it." I watch the fear creep back into Portia's eyes. Why is everyone so afraid of me all the time?! It always seems to be when I'm trying to tell them something important, and then they wonder why I get angry! "Bloody hell, Portia! Cath was my girlfriend, okay? She was in a bad place mentally, and so was I, for different reasons, and yeah, things did get a bit fucked up – we both lost our ways a bit, and no relationship is perfect – but I did love her, and it does take two to tango. You know? Yes, she's the one who died, and I suppose it's a natural thing, in a kind of evolutionary way, that people take the woman's word over the man's when there's … conflict in a relationship, but she wasn't a fucking saint, you know? She had her secrets. It was her who called out the wrong name when we were having sex once – although she was too pissed to remember that she'd done it – and it was her responsibility to stop drinking when she was on those anti-depressants, and it was her choice not to talk to me and try to work things through. I was trying to help her! I was the one who said we could move up to Manchester together, so she'd have some support when she started university; I put in for a transfer and everything! Fucking hell!"

I've been pacing around, and now there's nothing within reach to punch, so I just spin round and bring my hands up through my hair. Portia hasn't moved a muscle, so I grab my packet of fags and spark one up. Fuck vaping – it's for snowflakes!

She laughs. I must have said the last bit out loud. "You going to offer me one, then?" she says. I toss her the packet, and try to throw up the sash, but I locked it, so I bash my knuckles on the top half of the window.

"Fucking hell!" I slide the catch round and open the window. There are a few piss-heads stumbling up Angel Hill, and there's a queue outside the Chinese. Apparently, they still do chips and gravy there. What the fuck is wrong with people?!

"So, Cath's the one you were supposed to have murdered, then?"

"That's a very badly constructed sentence, Portia, but, yes, I did time for a crime I didn't commit, and even though I was cleared of all charges, everyone still hates me."

"Mud sticks."

"Yes. So I like to chip away at it and get to the truth."

"Literally as well as metaphorically." She means my being a palaeontologist.

"Yes."

"Taxidermy is a bit fucked up, though." She pauses, chokes a bit on her cigarette. "And threatening someone with it is *really* fucked up." She pauses again, exhales, meets my eyes. "Just saying."

"What?"

She says nothing, just stares at me with those lovely level eyes.

"Sorry, Portia, I seem to be missing something here."

"You said you were going to kill me and cut me up and disembowel me and stuff me."

"What?!"

She looks scared again, but doesn't break eye contact, just repeats the sentence.

"I never said anything of the sort, and you know it!" What the fuck is she on?! This is so fucking typical of the way people treat me!

"Well, no, you never said it in words, but you implied it."

"No, I didn't!"

"You did! When you were on about everyone just trying

to work things out and get to the truth in their own way –"

"What the FUCK, Portia?!" I throw my cigarette butt out of the window and smash my hand on the sill. There's a crack, and some paint flakes off. "You honestly thought I was going to … ugh! That's disgusting! How the - ? Anyway, I wouldn't even know where to start!"

"But you did Noel."

"I … what?! You think I killed and stuffed Noel?! Fucking hell! I won him on a fucking tombola!"

"What?"

"I was at a charity market stall fete type thing, raising money for the art therapy room at The Beeches!"

"What's The Beeches?"

"It's the psych ward at the RD and E! Cath got treated there, and so did her best mate!"

"You won a stuffed seagull on a tombola?!"

"A gull, not a 'seagull', Portia, but, yes! An old lady had donated him, I happened to pick his number, and I didn't have the heart not to take him home, poor bugger!"

We are in hysterics for about half an hour, and I tell you what - it's a fucking relief. The pizza arrives, with a bottle of Coke, and the guy says that because he was so late, they've chucked in some free cheesy garlic bread. Portia and I are sitting side by side on the sofa, laughing, stuffing our faces with junk food, drinking vodka – there was no Champagne at Jerry's, and the wines were crap - and Coke, and it's great until she says, "Fucking hell, Rich! You need to work on your social interaction techniques! I mean, do you have, like Asperger's or something?!"

When I pause and look at her, it's like someone's chucked a bucket of ice down her spine. Very quietly, she says "Is Cath the one who died in your bath? Hang on, and wasn't her best friend called Kayleigh? As in Liam's mum?"

We stare at each other in silence, frozen. Someone bangs on the door.

Liam

"Liam? Liam Brookes?"

I raise my head in the direction of the voice. "Yeah?"

The man speaks into a crackling walkie-talkie.

"Liam, my name's Darren. I'm a paramedic. I'm here to help you." He crouches close to me on the damp grass. Why am I on the grass? "Hi, Liam." He smiles. I return the smile.

"I don't feel very well." My voice sounds funny.

"I know you don't. Can you tell me what happened?"

"Umm. My head." I can't remember. "I can't remember."

I hear a car pulling up. "Look at those lights!" They're bright blue. Pretty. A car door slams. Someone is coming over. "Who's that?" I'm scared.

"Liam, this is Cerys. She's a paramedic, too."

Cerys is pulling something out of a holdall.

"Hi, Liam," she says, "I'm just going to pop this blanket round you to keep you warm." They help me sit up.

"I'm all wet!" I start laughing, then wince when Cerys pulls the shiny blanket round my arm.

"Have you got pain anywhere other than your arm, Liam?" she asks.

"My head. Ouch!" I wince again, and when I bring my hand back from my hair, it's all dark and sticky.

"Okay, Liam – easy!" says Darren. "Are you able to stand?"

I stumble as I'm trying to stand, and Darren supports my shoulders, which hurts my arm. I feel very heavy. Slow. "I'm tired."

With Darren and Cerys on either side of me, we pick our way along the grass. The car turns out to be an ambulance. It's very bright in the ambulance. They've both put one of those pale blue disposable facemasks on. Cerys has a kind of iPad. I am sitting on a long seat with white sheets. "Where's Darren gone?"

"He's driving the ambulance, Liam."

"Are we going to hospital?" someone asks. I'm so tired, I curl up on the white sheet and close my eyes.

"Are you an angel?" There's a woman sitting near me. She has a kind smile and very red lips. She laughs.

"No, Liam. I'm not an angel. I'm Sarah – I'm a nurse. I noticed you waking up, and thought I'd sit with you until you did."

I sit up. I am in a hospital gown, and I'm clean. Gingerly, I reach my hand up to touch my head. There's a bandage. My head is sore. "I've got a cracking headache!"

"You've fractured your skull, Liam. Can you remember what happened?"

Can I remember what happened? My brain feels foggy. "Not really."

Sarah's face is a picture of concern. "You have bruising on the left side of your head, but the fracture is on the right." It's a leading statement. Through the gap in the curtains, I can see a couple of police officers. They're shifting from foot to foot, obviously waiting for something.

"I was on the beach with P-" I stop. Portia.

"With who, Liam?"

I need to think about this. I don't know what's happened to Portia. She must be with Uncle Richard. I should tell the police what happened so they can find her, but if I do that, Uncle Richard will be back in prison, and if go goes back to prison, he probably won't come out again, and he definitely won't tell me who my real dad is, and it *was* all my fault for throwing the ammonite – I *know* he's got issues, and I provoked him. But more than that, he's a brilliant palaeontologist, and he did ask for my help, and imagine what would happen if we found a new species! Or even better, proof that it was actually the meteor that killed off the dinosaurs?! But then he raped my mum. But did he? He was cleared of all charges twenty years ago, and Mum was a psycho – she was literally schizophrenic - even Dad admits that. And I know Uncle Richard has a power thing, so maybe he said he'd raped my mum just to make me angry. I can't work him out. He's like Jekyll and Hyde. It's like that whole thing with that footballer who's been accused of rape – if you stop him playing football because of it to make him an example and do the morally right thing, you then fuck things up for the whole team, all the fans, and probably France's chances of qualifying for the World Cup, too. And it might not even be true. It's supposed to be *innocent until proven guilty,* isn't it? And you can't trust women – my own girlfriend's a case in point! You can't trust anyone, so all you can do is make the right choice for you. But then, what if –

I'm sick. Projectile vomit all over Sarah, all over my bed, all over the floor. "Oh, my God. I'm so sorry," I mumble as another motherload spurts out.

"Well, that's sorted that little dilemma out!" Sarah says, helping me into the high-backed chair next to my bed. "You are definitely not well enough to speak to the police!"

"The police? -"

"It's okay, Liam, it's not a problem. You just take it easy for now. I'll get you another gown, but your dad will be in later with some fresh clothes, and toiletries –"

"My dad?"

"Yes. We called him when you came in, but he's not allowed into the hospital before general visiting hours. I'll be back in a minute." She walks out with my sheets under one arm. I can't believe how quickly she's stripped the bed.

Richard

"Open this fucking door now, Richard!"

It's my dear, darling brother, Adam. Liam's dad – or so he thinks.

Portia freezes with fear again, and I'm not sure that it's not because I hit her boyfriend and left him for dead on the seashore, and here she is laughing and joking, getting pissed and sharing a pizza with me. I can't wait to see how Adam reacts. This is why I rarely watch the TV – truth is so much more exciting than fiction! I shoot Portia a wide grin, and head down the stairs.

Adam is still shouting and hammering on the door – with both hands, it sounds like - and I wonder if I can get the timing right so that he falls through the door when I open it. I'm jubilant when things transpire even better than I imagined – he stumbles into the hall and hits me in the face!

"What the FUCK did you do to my son?!"

I yank him in by the shoulder and shove him so I can slam the front door.

"What the fuck did you do to my face?!" I counter, with a grin.

"You cunt. You absolute fucking cunt! Why did you even have to come back here, eh? We would have been fine – everyone would have been fine! – if you'd just stayed away! But, no, you had to come and spread your poison over everything and everyone! Kayleigh's dead, Cath's dead and you left my fucking son for dead – you're evil, Richard! You're –"

"I'm going to stop you right there, brother," I say, calmly pushing him into the wall and sealing his mouth with my hand. "Firstly, my girlfriend, Catherine, was severely depressed, and she slit her wrists in my bath and left me to clean it up and take the flack. Secondly, I was in prison when Kayleigh was murdered by that psycho, so I clearly had nothing to do with that. Thirdly, what on earth are you talking about?! I haven't seen Liam since he was a toddler. I mean, what? He must be twenty, twenty-four by now?"

"He's twenty-three and you fucking know it!" Adam forces muffled words out through my hand. "I know you met up with him while he was in Liverpool! I mean, fuck, you probably even taught him, didn't you? You did! You did, didn't you?! You knew exactly who he was!"

To be fair to him, Adam is right. I'd been in my office at the University of Liverpool, a week or so before the freshers were due to arrive, in October 2018. It had been one of those flat, grey days when there was not even a breath of wind, so the dying leaves clung onto their branches like deflated balloons, and you needed the lights on inside all day. I'd been sipping the cooling dregs of my takeaway coffee, scrolling through my emails, and had come across my list of new students for the coming term. 'Liam Brookes 'had jumped out and metaphorically slapped me in the face, but then as both names are common, I'd managed to push the knowledge down. Until I'd seen him standing in the queue outside the Invisible Windmill Factory one Friday night. I'd have called it intuition, if I'd believed in that shit, but as I was walking home from Murphy's Bar, something other than the lack of clothing on the girls had made me really look at the people in the queue. And there he was. Same Superdry T-shirt, skinny jeans like cling film round his gangly legs. Nan always said that the Lord moves in mysterious ways. On the Monday morning, I strode up to the lectern, brought my notes up on my laptop – not that I needed them – and glanced up at my new students. This close up, what I saw made me gasp. There was Liam, near the back, in a seat on the end of an aisle, wearing a denim jacket this time. He really was the absolute spitting image of someone I used to know.

After the initial shock, I'd introduced myself, done the *welcome to the University of Liverpool Archaeology*

Department bit, and given my lecture. The students seemed keen, and I was looking forward to the seminar on Wednesday. Many of them thanked me on the way out, and when I saw Liam jogging down the steps towards me, I presumed he was going to do the same, and made the split decision not to tell him we were related. Yet. Partly because I now knew that Adam was not his father.

It turned out that the boy was full of surprises. He hissed, "Long time, no see, *Uncle*. I know who you are, and I know what you did, so you'd better be nice to me," and made to stalk off.

He sounded just like his dad. I laughed, caught him by the strap of his rucksack, and spun him back round to face me. "But do you know who *you* are?" I asked, "Because I really don't think that I'm your uncle!"

And now, confronted with my brother, Adam, screaming at me that I know his son, and have seen him recently, assaulted him, and put him in hospital, I say, calmly and clearly, "Do *you* know exactly who he is? Or should I say, exactly *who s* he is?"

Also, I now knew who it was that had written 'cunt 'on my front door.

Eskwich, February 2019

Portia

I'm sitting on the school fence, waiting for Liam's bus to come in. It's almost Valentine's Day, and he's coming back from uni to see me. And to check on his dad. I hadn't liked the expression on his face as he'd said it (we'd Facetimed) – it was more like it was a chore to him, like having to do his laundry, or clean out the fish tank or something. And that was the first time I actually thought, *he's seeing someone else.* As soon as I'd thought it, I berated myself, because I knew that he went to uni to study, not just to escape like everyone else. He'd always known what he'd wanted to do - since he was about six years old. He'd told me he'd made his dad put up dinosaur wallpaper and get him a dino duvet set, even though Adam had been reluctant to because dinosaurs were his brother, Richard's, passion and he fucking hated Richard with every bone in his body, although he hadn't told Liam exactly why until Liam had said he wanted to go to Liverpool to study archaeology. So, yeah, Liam had always had a passion for the past, and had always had a career plan. We'd be at parties with our mates, everyone all pissed up and high, dancing, singing, getting off with each other and that, and Liam would be there sat in a corner somewhere, or under a table, or sitting cross-legged on someone's kitchen worktop, reading other people's theses and looking up pictures of fossils on his phone. That's partly how he got the nickname 'Bony – 'that and the fact that he's built like a string bean.

I think all these things, sitting on the school fence, looking at the dead hedgehog, puffing on my vape, watching old people extricate themselves from buses with those stupid pull-along trolley things and bumble their ways back down to the bungalows on Blackmore Road, some of them couples, wrinkled and ancient as fuck, but still holding hands, and then I berate myself again for being so fucking deluded, to think that my boyfriend was all about the noble beliefs – he was 240-odd miles away, of course he was shagging around, everyone did it, his own dad had warned him about it, told him to split up with me before he went … I spend my days and nights in a state of constant turmoil – what we have is either pure and holy and above the ordinary, or we're exactly the same as everybody else and I'm living in a dream - there's no middle ground. Maybe I'm just overthinking it all. But if he *is* cheating on me, why am I wasting all this time thinking about him and waiting on a fence in the cold for hours, for a bus that he might not even be on, when I should be doing my own studying, planning my own career. My best mate, Chelsea, was right – love is just a distraction – a coping mechanism gone haywire. Chemicals. I need a drink.

I think about calling Chelse and seeing if she wants to meet me in The Riverboat, but then I remember she's working at Costa now, just about every shift she can do so she can save up for that trip to Dubai she's always on about. She doesn't seem to want to do anything more than work, buy clothes, and get pissed up at the weekend, but then I guess she'll end up marrying Declan and having kids and that will be that – she'll be sorted. I can't see that happening for me and Liam somehow. I'm literally just sitting on the fence.

I could go up to Manchester and try and make this thing work with Liam, but something tells me that he wants to be left to find his own path now … and he probably wants to share a house with Atlantis and his intellectual mates. Forget his roots, make some money, finally be free of his dad. He hasn't told me, but I know he's got the opportunity to go and study in China for a year – I checked his course out on their website when he was thinking about where to apply to - and there's no way he won't take it. I expect he'll go with Atlantis, and she can make her films or find a cure for cancer or be a supermodel, or whatever she's trying to do, there. I take my vape out of my pocket and take a long drag, wishing it was something stronger that would either knock me out or give me an epiphany.

I'm almost out of vape juice. I ought to cut it out and stop smoking all together, but it's still that thing my mum always said, about having that five minutes out to think, especially because now you can't smoke indoors like you could in the old days. I shove my vape back into its home in my jacket pocket, and drop off the fence. I want to move the hedgehog out of the road, but there are no sticks about or anything. I've just decided that I'm going to nudge it to the kerb so it won't get splattered, but then a crow swoops down and starts picking at it again. It's best I leave it where it is so the crow can get some food. That's the only form of reincarnation I believe in.

I kind of salute the carcass, like you do when you see a lone magpie – for luck and to bless it, if that makes any sense - and then head off down Lazenby Road. I used to go to Wilcombe School. It's where I met Chelsea. We smoked our first fags together behind the bike sheds. It's a cliché, but where else were we going to do it? There's nowhere that isn't overlooked by houses anymore, and even though the town's expanded, everyone's mum and dad still drinks in The Riverboat, so word still gets round that way, if they don't see it online first. I hate these 'spotted 'sites – it's an invasion of privacy.

The wind's picked up and it blows my hood down. I zip up my jacket, pull the vape from my pocket on autopilot, remember that it's empty, and decide to stop at the corner shop and get some more juice and a Bounty. I haven't eaten breakfast today, but that's just laziness, not because I'm on a diet. Although, I'm sure Bountys are one of your five a day.

I can't help myself looking, furtively, in everyone's gardens as I go past. Some of them are neat, with cyclamen and bedding plants in pots; some have been paved over and are now more carparks than gardens; a couple of them have old fridges on the lawn, piles of fag butts around the gates. Some of these people have lived here for decades, from when they bought their council houses. Some of them are young couples or single mums on Universal Credit – you can tell because they've got those trampolines taking up half the lawn, the rest of it littered with varying sizes of bikes, and the front door's always open.

The most interesting house, though, is the one with the paved front garden with all the statues in it. It's weird, and freaks me out a bit, even now. When Chelsea and I were kids, there were loads of rumours about it. One was that the old duck who lives there had too many cats, and someone called the RSPCA on her because they were shitting on their lawn and killing all the birds that came to their bird table. The lady was one of those 'crazy cat ladies', and lived for her cats, even though the house stunk and there were loads of catfights because they couldn't get away from each other, and she couldn't bear to have them taken away, so she killed them all and buried them in her garden. She put a statue over every grave, and she did it in the front garden so that it was one in the eye for the neighbour who'd dobbed her in. Other people said she killed her husband and chopped him up and then put statues over the holes so there wouldn't be a smell and a fox wouldn't dig them up in the night. But when all those cats started going missing, everyone reckoned she'd lured them in with chicken, then killed them, eaten them, and put the bones under the statues. So, the statue of the angel was on top of someone's Bengal cat called Angel, the rabbit was over the moggie from number 7, called Bunny, and so on. The ones under the gnomes hadn't had names, or she didn't know their names – that's why there were so many of them. This was all freaky when we were kids, but part of us knew it was just people talking shit – everyone makes up stories about women who lived alone. The stigma hasn't gone, which is why I find myself wondering if I ought to find another boyfriend and get married, so I'm not single in my thirties – but for me, it was more than that, because of the statue of the Italian clown. My aunty used to live up here, before she divorced her husband for shagging around, and she'd had a pure white, fluffy cat, with David Bowie eyes, called Scaramouche. He was one of the cats that – or is it 'who', if you know the cat and their name? - had gone missing, and I always got a shiver when I passed by. Which I did every time I went up to see Liam. I could have gone a different way, but something kept pulling me up Lazenby Road, even though I still don't get why she didn't just eat the chicken instead of the cats.

"Oh, shit, sorry! I was miles away!" I say to the person I've bumped into, coming out of the shop when I was going in.

"Portia?"

I stare into the face of the person who's spoken, blushing. Only to find that he is blushing redder than me.

"Portia'?! Is that what I am to you now? A fucking stranger?!"

"Shit, Porche! Sorry! I was miles away, too!" Liam puts his hands on my shoulders, but I shrug him off and back away, turning and almost running down Halsbury Road.

"Porche!" Liam is coming after me, so I break into a sprint, the tears stinging my eyes as I go. But I'm not fast enough. "Porche!" Liam grabs my arm and pulls me round to face him. "Jesus, Porche! What the fuck?!"

"What do you mean, 'what the fuck'?! Bastard! I was waiting for you, like I said I would, for fucking ages and you never showed! You were trying to avoid me! Is *she* in the corner shop?! Is that what it is?!" I'm crying loads now, and I really need to blow my nose and I can't find a tissue but, fuck it! He doesn't give a shit about me anymore so what does it matter?!

"Porche! What the hell are you on about?!" Liam wraps

me in a hug, and I just dissolve into his shoulder, hating myself for it. We stand like that for a long time – I think because we know we'll have to say something to each other when we break away, and neither of us knows what to do. As my breathing returns to normal, I remember I have a tissue in my jeans pocket, so I tidy up my face and wipe the snot and tears off Liam's puffer jacket. I ought to break out of this embrace now, tell him it's over, walk off and get on with my life, but because of the smell of him, and the fact that this is so familiar, and I've missed it, I find myself snuggling my face back into his shoulder, and then going over all the possible courses of action again, in my head. This is maddening!

"Look, Porche, I've left all my stuff outside the shop. I need to go back and get it before someone nicks it." He's stroking my hair. He stops and kisses my head. "Are you going to come with me, or –"

"Yeah. Yeah, okay." We turn round and walk back to the shop. "I need to get some vape juice, anyway." Liam laughs. I lift my head now I can feel my face has gone back to a normal colour, and I can see a pile of rucksacks, dumped in the middle of the pavement. When I go into the shop, I'm the only one in there bar the girl on the till, and I know her because she's worked here forever. I feel a bit embarrassed.

Liam, rucksacks now back over each shoulder, raises his eyebrows at me when I come out. "Yeah, yeah, alright, sorry." I look at the ground. We stand there for a beat, still not knowing what to do.

"So," he says. "Are you coming back to my dad's, or –"

Liam and I retrace my route along Lazenby Road, in silence. We're walking quite close together, and I start swinging my right arm in case he wants to hold my hand, but both of his are stuffed in his pockets. When we reach the house with the freaky front garden, he points vaguely in the direction of the statues and says, "So, what's your theory, then?"

I presume he's joking – just because it's something neutral to say - so I give a kind of snort of derision and glance up at him. I'm surprised to see him staring me earnestly in the face. "What?! You're joking, aren't you?" I say it gently because I can't tell what he's thinking.

"Actually, no I'm not. We used to joke about it when we were at school, but I reckon she's a cat killer. At least."

I stop walking, and look at Liam, wide-eyed.

"Come on," he says, kind of shoving me back into walking again, "we can't stop here - she might see us."

I actually laugh at this. "Seriously, Lee, you think this hundred-year-old old duck's going to come out and shoot us with a fucking AK or something?! Or – what? – she'll lure us inside with a bag of pick n 'mix and bake us in a pie?!"

Liam grabs my arm so hard it hurts, even through the padding of my jacket. "What the fuck, Lee?!" He marches me up the road.

We're at the corner of Marshall Close before he lets go. I say 'let's go – 'what he actually does is kind of throw my arm away, so I'm propelled forward, and stumble off the kerb and into the road.

"This is half the problem with us, Porche!" he spits, looking daggers at me. "You think everything's a fucking joke!"

"What are you talking about?!"

"You do things and say things because – I don't know – because you're trying to be cool, or something, like you're still fourteen! It never occurs to you for one minute that you might actually be hurting people!" He pauses for a beat, then adds, "You don't know what people can be like," and slopes off down the road and round the corner. His dad's house is right at the end, by the entrance to the canal.

His head's down, and he kicks a Coke can that's lying in

the road. I think he was aiming for one of the garages, but the can just rattles along the gravel for a bit and gets stuck in a patch of dandelions growing up through a pothole. He stops, looks at his dad's house, then walks right past it and onto the canal tow path. He disappears to the left, and I run to catch him up.

"Liam!" I shout at his back, but he carries on. "Liam!" He speeds up, goes under the foot bridge, and then stops and sits on the little stump of a bench that's just on the other side.

"Fuck's sake! Liam!" As I'm plonking myself down next to him, he nearly knocks me off taking the rucksacks off his back. He stretches out his long legs so he can pull his baccy and a lighter out of his jeans pocket. I reach for my vape and try to sort it out, but it's tricky because I think the coil's going.

We sit in silence, smoking for a bit. A bunch of ducks paddle over, jump clumsily out of the water, and waddle up to us, quacking. "Sorry, guys – we've got no bread," I say, quietly.

"You know you're not supposed to feed ducks bread, don't you?"

"What?"

"It's no good for them. It bloats them right out so they don't bother going for their natural food that's got all the goodness in it. It's the perfect example of killing with kindness."

"Oh. No, I didn't know." At least he's talking to me. "My grandma used to buy a loaf of bread specially for them, and she used to take me up here in the school holidays when Mum and Dad were at work so we could feed them. I used to love it. It was kind of our treat."

Liam snorts and coughs a bit on his rollie. "Yeah, well, that's old ladies for you, isn't it?" he says. It's not a question.

"So why are you so uptight about the 'Garden of the

Dead'?" I say, realising as soon as I've said it, that Liam isn't going to like it.

He snorts again, takes a long drag, and blows the smoke out slowly, shaking his head. "'Garden of the fucking Dead'," he mutters. "You know that saying, *there s no smoke without fire?*"

"Yeah, of course I do! It's a cliché. Like *mud sticks.*" A thought comes to me, and I can't help but add, "It's something an old lady would say." I can't help the smirk, either. Sometimes it feels good to wind him up. Sometimes he needs to remember that he's not the only person to come out of this town who's intelligent.

"Look, Portia," he says, "you're really doing my head in today. I was on that fucking train for five hours, and all I could think about was how I couldn't wait to see you again, and all you've done is act like a fucking twat."

He seems to be on the verge of tears. He's smoked his rollie very quickly, and he drops what's left of it, stamps on it, crushes it into the ground, and makes to roll another one. He's staring at the bullrushes. I remember coming up here once with Chelsea. We used to play around here a lot when we were kids – everyone did. One summer we'd come up here just to mooch along, kicking up the red dust, telling each other our secrets and eating pick n 'mix, but we got to a point where all the water was covered in lily-pads, and there were fucking frogs everywhere! I mean, like, everywhere! It was gross! Chelsea tried to make her way through them, but they were hopping all over each other and she nearly squashed one, so she started picking them up and chucking them back in the water. I just stood there, trying not to throw up. I can't remember what happened in the end. We must have just gone home.

I'm staring at the ground, now, making patterns in the dust with my boots. Liam's silent. I remember another day - it must have been about teatime - Chelsea's mum rang up and told my mum that Chelse had gone missing, and if I knew where she could have gone. Chelse had been pissed off at school that day, but that was nothing unusual – we were pre-teens, all full of hormones – one of us was usually in a mood about something or another. Anyway, Chelsea's mum had called the police, but they said they couldn't do anything until she'd been missing twenty-four hours, or something, and her mum had been, like, *this is my twelve-year-old daughter, we're talking about! A young girl missing after dark, when all the druggies and perverts about! Get off your fat, lazy arses and find her! I pay your fucking wages!* 'I pay your fucking wages. 'I'd had no idea what she was talking about – after all, she worked on the tills in Tesco – she wasn't like a big police chief or anything. In the end, a whole group of mums and dads and her friends went looking for Chelse, and I said had anyone tried up the canal, and they'd found her, hiding under the foot bridge. She'd barricaded herself in with fallen branches and stuff so you couldn't have seen her unless you'd known where to look, and she'd been sat there with a can of Coke and a tube of barbeque Pringles. Everyone was asking why she'd done it and made everyone worry so much, but she wouldn't tell them anything more than *I just felt like running away,* even though her mum was stood there crying. I'd talked to her in private afterwards, but she wouldn't tell me, either. I'd been pretty hurt, because we told each other everything. Or at least I thought we did.

"A cliché is a cliché because it happens so much," Liam says, softly. He's still staring at the bullrushes. He opens his mouth and then shuts it again, and his chin wobbles a bit, so I touch his arm, and he looks at me and smiles. "I do love you, you know, Portia," he says. "that's why you hurt me so much. I wouldn't care if I didn't care. If that makes sense."

"Liam, what's going on?" This feels like the start of a break-up conversation. My mouth wobbles a bit, too.

"You know I used to do my paper-round around here?"

"Yeah?" Why isn't he talking about us?

"Well, you see things early in the morning, when there's no one about. And I used to see her – that lady with … with the Garden of the Dead, if that's how you want to refer to it. She'd be putting out all these saucers of milk and chicken – you know, the fine china ones that only old people have – and of course, cats being crepuscular, they were all up and about, and they used to smell it and come over to her and get an early breakfast there."

I don't know what 'crepuscular 'means, but I don't want to stop him now that he's in mid-flow, so I make a mental note to Google it later.

"If she saw me coming, she'd come up and say *hello* and take the paper from me, so I didn't have to get off my bike and walk up to her door, she said, but one day I'd slept in, so I was late. She wasn't in the garden when I got there, and although the bowls were out – she used to dot them around her garden – most of them were empty, and I couldn't see any cats. I left my bike in front of her gate and walked up to stuff the paper in her letterbox –"

Liam's smoked his second rollie, and he's just sitting there, fiddling with his packet of Rizlas. He's looking at the ground now, so I squeeze his arm, and sit closer to him. He smiles, then looks at me quickly, before staring at the bullrushes again.

"I heard this weird noise," he says, and he pauses again. "Coming from inside. Like a screech. It gave me the fucking shivers, and when I opened the letterbox to put the paper in, I –"

"Alright, Liam?! I thought I heard your dulcet tones! Hiya, Portia! Are you two coming inside, or what?!"

It's Liam's dad, Adam. His face is too cheery. We both know he's been drinking.

Royal Devon and Exeter Hospital, January 2022

Liam

"Oh, my fucking God, Liam!" Dad appears at the end of my bed and dumps a bulging Tesco bag on my feet. Sarah's replacement is doing my obs, so Dad bustles round to the other side of my bed, rips off his disposable facemask and surprises me by gripping me by the shoulder.

"Richard did this to you, didn't he?" Dad looks like his heart is breaking. I've never seen him like this before. "I'll fucking kill him, Lee, I swear it!" The nurse is on the side of my bed with the inevitable upright chair, and Dad looks all over the place for something to plonk himself on. In the end, he just kind of stands there, shifting his weight from foot to foot like a tennis player waiting for their opponent to serve.

The nurse takes the thermometer out from under my tongue and studies it, allowing me to speak.

"Hi, Dad! I –"

"I'm sorry, sir, but I'm going to have to ask you to put your face covering back on," the nurse says through her own mask. "We're still in the middle of a pandemic, you know." While Dad's reeling at the shock of being told off by this tiny woman who's probably younger than me, she turns her brown eyes to mine saying softly, "Liam, if this is true and you know the person who did this to you, you really should speak to the police –" She glances towards the nurses 'station to see if the coppers are still there.

"No! No, it's fine … my dad's got the wrong end of the stick. Dad, listen, I was fossil-hunting and I slipped on the rocks, that's all – it was my own stupid fault!" I look at them both. The nurse stands there, Velcro blood-pressure wrap in hand; Dad shaking his head, removes his hand from my shoulder. She knows damned well my story is inconsistent with my injuries; he knows it's bollocks because he's got this in-built lie-detector. He just stands there, picking at his knuckles. It's amazing how much people can convey with their eyes when most of the rest of their face is covered.

The nurse raises her eyebrows and wraps the blood-pressure thing around my arm, making me wince. "I'm sorry, Liam, I know it's sore. I'd do it on your other arm, but, you know, social-distancing!" She smiles at my dad, who glares back.

"I was told I could come in today to drop some clothes off and see my boy!" he hisses through his mask. "I didn't sleep all bloody night, I –"

"Okay, Mr Brookes," she says. "I'm sorry. It's been a long night. I didn't mean to be rude." The sincerity of the apology is evident in her gaze, and Dad nods. She squeezes the puffer thing until the wrap around my arm becomes tight to the point of discomfort, and just when it feels like my arm is going to explode, she releases the pressure and stares at the green digital numbers on the monitor until the contraption finishes hissing. I look at her NHS ID lanyard, Her name's Ellie. She looks about twelve in her photo.

"Okay, Liam," she says, smiling. "It seems that my machine is playing silly-buggers! Would you mind standing up? I'll take your blood-pressure again, just to check."

"Umm, yeah. Okay."

A nurse's smile is an enigma. It's kind, but weirdly ominous, because I'm always thinking that, obviously, they need to smile to put you at ease, but that could be over-compensation – like they're really thinking *bloody hell! I need to check this with the doctor!* Also, they have to be kind because they're helping people who are desperate and can't help themselves, but then it is their vocation – nursing isn't an I'll-flip-burgers-until-something-better-turns-up sort of job. I mean, you have to study for it. And go through what most people would consider hell, on a daily basis. They're altruistic. They should be paid more – Covid or no

Covid. But they probably know it, so when they smile at you and say, *okay, don t worry, let s just get you cleaned up,* I always wonder if they're really thinking, *two hours, just two more hours and then I can go home. Fuck cooking, I m going to grab a Maccy D s and then go to bed. Please, please don t let there be an emergency ...*

Ellie moves her obs trolley out of the way and holds her arm out to support me as I ease myself out of bed. My fingers grip so hard I make white marks on her brown skin, and I apologise, at which she smiles again, saying, "It's okay, don't worry."

"Oh my God, Liam! Look at your legs!" Dad's eyes, staring at my bare legs, well up. He runs his hands through his hair, and spins so his back is towards us, shaking his head. When I have both feet firmly on the floor, I pull down my hospital gown as far as I can, but glance down my body. My legs are black and blue, scrawny, hairy sticks, and my feet are Hobbity. A shiver of revulsion passes through me, my head starts banging again. I feel like I'm going to pass out, but Ellie steadies me with surprisingly strong hands on my shoulders, looking me right in the eyes until she can tell that I feel better.

"You okay?" she asks, redundantly. I nod and smile, embarrassed that she's seen my legs, wondering what the hell Portia sees in me. Portia. I need to get out of here as soon as I can. I need to find her. But the police could do it better than me. But if I tell the police, Richard will go back to prison, and then he'll never tell me who my real dad is. I imagine him, sneering at me over the table in the visiting room, gloating. *I know something you don t know.*

"Don't look so frightened, Liam," Ellie says, kindly, removing the cuff from my arm. "Your blood-pressure's fine. Sometimes the fact that you've been lying down for ages can make it read low but - believe me – your obs are all good! I know the doctors want to keep you in for a while longer, just to make sure you're okay, but you'll be going home soon, don't worry!" She supports me while I climb back into bed, pulling the over-sheet and powder-blue crocheted blanket nearly up to my chin, to hide my repulsive body.

Ellie puts the obs trolley to one side and pushes over the portable cupboard with the computer on top that every nurse seems to be working off. She types something in, then stares at the screen. "How's your pain right now, Liam. I could give you some more paracetamol now, if you'd like, or codeine –"

"No! Not codeine! It does messes me up!" I blurt, sitting up suddenly, sparking another blinding headache. "I'll have some paracetamol, though, if that's alright?"

"Of course!" Ellie rummages in the cupboard of tricks, and presents me with two thick, round white tablets in a paper thimble. I swig them back, like I would a shot of Jager, but they stick in my throat. Bloody paracetamol! They don't have the shiny coating that ibuprofen do! I kind of gag, and Ellie springs into action, pouring me a glass of water from the jug on my table. I take it from her, glaring at Dad, who's pissing himself with laughter.

"Thanks," I splutter, handing the glass back to her, feeling my cheeks burn with embarrassment. She smiles, then turns away, pushing the obs trolley with one hand, pulling the drugs cupboard with the other. "Five minutes, Mr Brookes," she calls over her shoulder. "Your son needs to rest."

As soon as Ellie's gone, Dad whips round to the other side of my bed and drops into the chair. Pulling his mask off again, he says, "Look, Liam, I'm not bloody stupid. I *know* Richard did this to you. In fact, I'm fucking insulted that you'd lie to me, but we'll leave that, coz you're in a bad way. Why don't you just shop him?! Then we'll be rid of him, and he can rot in prison like he deserves to!" He's angry, but it's mostly concern. It occurs to me that this is the nearest he's ever come to saying he loves me. It almost makes me cry. Dad must have noticed, because he reaches for the Tesco bag and scrabbles around in it.

"Don't get everything out, Dad, just dump it in my locker thing for now. I'll have a shower and put some proper clothes on later –"

"'Thanks for bringing my stuff in, Dad,'" he says, sarcastically.

"Oh, sorry! Thanks, Dad. Sorry –"

"Don't worry about it. Aha! Here it is! I bought you a present." He holds a punnet of red grapes triumphantly aloft like they're the fucking Crown Jewels or something.

I laugh. "Seriously, Dad, you brought me some grapes?!"

"Of course! You're in hospital! I could hardly bring you a four-pack of Thatchers, could I?!"

"Fair point."

"And it doesn't look like Florence-the-younger's going to come round with a cup of tea any time soon, does it?!" He picks off a handful of grapes, one at a time and holds them out to me. I take one out of politeness, but when I bite into it, it's so cold and refreshing after the luke-warm water in my jug, in this stuffy ward, that I grab the lot out of his hand, and start stuffing them in my mouth.

"Hospital food's not up to much, then?" he jokes. We munch a few grapes, and then he turns serious.

"I went round his flat last night - Richard's flat I mean - right after the hospital called me – nearly hammered the cunt's door down." He flashes me his knuckles; fresh scabs forming over breaks in the bruising.

"Did you get in? Was Portia there?" Now I'm sitting forward, my eyes swimming.

Dad sighs. "It's always all about the bloody girl with us, isn't it, Lee?"

It's not a question, but I ask, "What do you mean?"

"Never mind, mate, never mind. Well, he wouldn't let me in any further than the hall, but I could see up the stairs and Portia poked her head round the banister – she's okay, mate! She's okay! I mean, it was obvious she didn't want me to let on that I'd seen her, but she gave me the thumbs-up. Actually, it smelt like they'd ordered a Dominoes, or something –"

He trails off as Ellie appears at the foot of my bed. "Right, Mr Brookes, I'm afraid I'm going to have to ask you to leave. And please wear your face-covering in the hospital – we all have to try to do our bit to avoid increasing infections." She doesn't say, *people are dying here, literally, you fucking irresponsible prick,* but she's thinking it.

Dad pulls his facemask from where he's shoved it in his back pocket. It's one of those disposable blue ones that you get in packs of ten for a fiver or something, and we all know that he's been wearing the same one since Boris told him he had to. At least he puts it over his nose as well as his mouth. Old people just don't get it – it's no wonder they're dying. Dad gets to his feet, saying, "I've put your phone charger in the bag, Lee. Give us a bell when they've said you can come home, and I'll pick you up." He hesitates before walking away. "Then we can have a proper chat about everything." His face is serious now. The 'everything 'was loaded. Richard's told him. He knows.

Portia

Once I've given Adam the thumbs-up behind Richard's back, I dive back onto the sofa, grab a slice of pizza, take a couple of bites out of it and then just sit still, holding it. When Richard comes back up the stairs, I want it to look like I was being quiet, trying to overhear their conversation. In actual fact, I do want to overhear their conversation, but all I get after the shouting is Richard laughing, saying "Or should I say exactly *who s* he is?"

There's a pregnant pause, then Adam says, "If you've got something to say, just fucking say it, Richard!" Another pause. I can imagine the brothers staring each other out in the dingy hallway. The silence goes on and on. Richard breaks it.

"Hmm, no, I don't think I *will,*" he says, and I can picture that malignant smile spreading over his face.

"You fucking cunt." That's Adam. "You're always on a fucking power-trip, aren't you? We both know Liam's mine. Mine and Kayleigh's. Remember Kayleigh? The girl you drove to her death –"

"Now who's on a power-trip?!" Richard laughs again. I feel sick. "We both know that Kayleigh was killed by your landlord – what was he called again? Will? – by Will's schizophrenic brother. Terrible tragedy. I'm sure he'll be in that secure unit for the rest of his life, which is a tragedy in itself. Another thing that's a tragedy is a cold Meat Feast Dominos. You can get away with having the vegetarian ones cold, but with meat, well, it's just not right. Meat's supposed to be warm. Unless you're a vulture, or a Tyrannosaurus Rex. Hmm. Anyway, goodbye, Adam. Do wish Liam well from me when you see him. I really do hope he makes a speedy recovery."

There's a bit of a scuffle, and the door slams.

Richard stomps up the stairs, straight past me, not even looking at me. It's like he's forgotten I'm here. I get up off the sofa and follow him along the corridor to the Room of Doom. He goes straight to the holdall on the table and pulls a laptop out of his bag.

I stand there in the doorway. He has his back to me and is scrolling through something. He seems to have found what he was looking for, because he stops and takes a notepad out of the laptop case. I can't see much, but I can see that there are loads of loose photos in inside.

"Are you going to eat that, or what?"

I gasp and almost drop the slice of pizza I didn't realise I was holding. It's like he has eyes in the back of his head.

"Sorry, I –"

"Thought I was stupid?"

"No! I just –"

"You don't trust me and you're wondering what I'm up to."

"Well, yes, actually!" He's still got his back to me, rifling through the photos. I step closer. At first, I think they're old, faded autopsy photographs, but then I realise it's ruddy mud, and bone. But not human bones. One of them looks like a crocodile's skull. An old one, with teeth missing. The next photo Richard examines is a close-up of one of the teeth. Then there's a photo of a man's fingers holding a tooth which must be about an inch thick and longer than his hand!

"What the fuck is that?!"

"It's the tooth of what I think is a new species of therapod, Portia."

"How do you know it's a new species?"

"I don't. That's why I said it was a *theory*."

I find myself pulling over the chair from the table with the microscope and the small tools, and sitting down next to Richard, my eyes fixed on the images.

"It's all about evolution, Portia. People are finding new

species all the time, from bones found years ago. It's easy to find a load of similar-looking bones in the same area and presume they're animals of the same species – it's logic, really, especially hundreds of years ago when 'fossil-hunters 'didn't have the technology we have today. And if you have no way of dating the bones, what are you supposed to think? But when you *do* have carbon-14 dating technology, the truth is revealed. And it's just nonsensical to think that an animal would be the same for millions of years without undergoing some sort of change."

Richard is rifling through his notebook now, searching for something. His writing is almost illegible to me – spiky and slanting to the left. He doesn't seem bothered what he writes with, either – it all looks rushed, like he's grabbed the nearest pen to him before he forgets what he's thinking. How he can find anything is a mystery to me.

"They've discovered three new species on the Isle of Wight in the last few months, and I want to discover the next. That's why I've taken a sabbatical."

"But surely there are palaeontologists working down there already?"

"There are indeed."

"And surely they have access to all the best places and all the equipment and stuff?"

"Yes."

"So why don't you just … I don't know … put in for a transfer, or give them a call, or something?" Richard's cheeks lift in a smirk – his eyes haven't left the notebook. "I mean, you've got tenure! You're respected in your field. And you're all on the same side!"

Richard huffs. "Are we, though, Portia? Are we though?" The questions are rhetorical, so I say nothing. He's clearly in the mood to talk, so I'm going to let him talk. "It seems to me that there isn't a human being on earth who's truly 'on the same side 'as someone else, Portia. It's basic evolution – we're all out for ourselves. If we weren't, we wouldn't have survived as a species. It's why you're sitting here, listening to me now, but really, you're wondering if I'm going to say anything that will help you get out of here.

"Things have never happened for me the way they should, Portia. Discovering a new species is not happening for me professionally, so I'm going to have to find it as a hobbyist. I'm going to walk along the Chines like a tourist. When I find something that's not useful to me, I'm going to carry it miles away from where I found it, just to confuse them. Or even take it home. Fuckers. I've had to fight for every damned thing I've achieved!"

Richard thumps the table, making me jump again, then hurls his notebook across the room, like a child having a tantrum.

"Nobody said life was easy." I say it before I realise what it reminds me of. Richard is glaring at me, so I smile and start humming that Coldplay song. He smiles back. Then he slams his fist into my face.

***Eskwich, 2021**

Portia

"So. You're fucking off to university and leaving me." Chelsea slides onto the green cushioned pew that runs along the wall of Costa and picks her caramel latte up off the table in one smooth move.

"I'm not *leaving* you, Chelse. I'm only –"

"Yes, I know what you're *only* doing!" She slurps the froth off her coffee. "Thanks for this, by the way."

"Yeah, don't worry about it. You can get the gin in when you come up to visit me!" I've got a hot chocolate, with squirty cream, marshmallows, and chocolate sprinkles on the top. I'm fishing the white marshmallows off with the stupidly long spoon they give you. It's not like you have to stir it – whoever puts sugar in one of these is going to have to buy shares in Fixodent. What's wrong with a normal spoon? Someone has to make all this shit!

"Oh, haha (!) I just don't know why you have to study *history* of all things! I mean, it's boring as fuck. Why couldn't you do something interesting, or at least relevant, like Chinese, or particle physics, or something?"

"Do you even know what particle physics is?!"

Chelsea laughs. "Well, no, but you know what I mean! History's obsolete – it's happened, gone! Move onto the next thing like computer science or climate … studies, or –"

"'Climate Studies'? I don't think that's even a thing!" I've started on the cream now. If Chelsea wasn't here, I'd have eaten the lot by now, and probably had a muffin as well.

"Fucking hell, Porche. You know what I mean! Everyone's like, *oh, we can only understand the future by looking to the past,* but no one ever learns from it! I mean, everyone goes round wearing poppies in November, but it doesn't stop wars, does it?"

"I think –"

"What's the point?! And you can't trust history anyway, because it's written by the winners! People like to edit it, for their own purposes. Like fake news. Propaganda, you know?"

"Bloody hell, Chelse. Have you got a tin foil hat in your bag?"

"Fuck off. I just think there are more useful things you could be studying, that's all. You've got the brains and the drive to do it, so you may as well do something that's actually going to help people. Otherwise, why don't you just work here? I mean, it's a regular wage, you could be manager one day, which means you could buy a house and that, and people are always going to want coffee, aren't they?" She takes a long drink of her latte, looking at me over the rim of the glass. She knows she's got a point.

"At least Liam's discovering dinosaurs, which is pretty cool. But what are you going to do with History, other than teach it to someone else? And you're going to come back with massive debts, and then find there are no decent jobs anyway! Employers want experience these days, not a bit of paper you could have got off the internet –"

That last bit does it for me. "Who says I'm coming back?"

Liam

Dad knows, and he knows that I know, too. Except, what do we know? Nothing for sure. But Uncle Richard's planted a seed and we're both wondering. When I was growing up, everyone said I was the spit of my dad – meaning Adam – but it might just have been because I had blond wavy hair, and because that's something you kind of feel you have to say to people when they present you with their baby. It's like they want you to find something of them in it; like you can't just appreciate the child for being a child, and a person in its own right. Lots of kids are born with one colour hair, and then it changes as they get older. And Mum's hair – by the photos, was bloody mental, so I could have got the waves from her. Although they've gone now. And it was brown. And then sometimes characteristics skip a generation – Prince Harry's hair being a case in point. Unless you believe the rumours. And now I'm back to me again.

Adam – why am I suddenly thinking of him as 'Adam'? – will always be my dad because he's the one who brought me up. To my knowledge, and his, until now, he *is* my dad. But, yeah, now it's been suggested to me that things might be different, I have to follow it up. It's no different to archaeology. Shit – I hope I don't literally have to dig something up. Or someone.

A young lad with a trolley has appeared at the foot of my bed. He looks even younger than Ellie, and his hospital uniform hangs off him. He's waiting for a response.

"Sorry? What –"

"Fucking masks," he mutters, pulling one ear free so I can see his mouth. "I said, 'Hi. D'you wanna cup of tea or something?" Then he pulls the elastic back round his ear. He actually looks better with it on – it covers most of his acne. Poor lad.

I smile at him. "Umm, yeah, okay. Can I get a coffee, please?"

"Milk and sugar?"

I'm tempted to say *no sugar thanks – I m sweet enough,* but I don't. "Yes, two sugars, please." He nods and gets to work, putting the milk in first. I want to pull him up on his bedside manner, but instead I say, "So, reckon Chelsea are going to beat Man City on Saturday?"

"No chance, mate," he says, "We're at home! We'll hammer 'em!" He hands me my coffee with a smile, then stops. "How did you know I support Man City?"

"The badge on your replica shirt shows through your uniform."

"Shit!" He looks down, tries to cover it up by scrunching his top.

"Don't worry about it, mate. It's a talking point. You'll find the day goes faster."

"Cheers, man," he says, and moves towards the guy in the bed next to me. "Hope you get well soon."

I drink my coffee and look around the ward. There are some proper sick people in here. The guy opposite me has the curtains round his bed again, but it doesn't stop the sound of him throwing up. Or the smell. Some bloke down the end can't stop groaning. The guy who's now getting a cup of tea that's mainly milk, has been down for scans or x-rays or whatever, about a million times. The nurses don't stop. The only rest they get is when they're standing next to your bed waiting for the monitors to do their thing. Occasionally a group of doctors will flounce in and start talking, and their presence is so … well, awesome, really, that it feels like they're giants in the room. And sometimes there are the students, trailing around with clip boards after a person in dark blue. They've all got masks on, the whole time. And it's baking in here. Like, it's so warm the air is thick with it. I imagine it full of red, spiky Covid particles,

their mass increasing exponentially. I've got to get out of
here.

When Ellie comes round to do my obs again, I ask her if
I can go home.

"Well, Liam, you have suffered a pretty serious head
injury. The doctors would like to keep you in for a while
longer – I explained that to you earlier."

"Yes, I know that, but … I mean … how are my obs?"

Ellie rips the black Velcro blood pressure cuff from my
arm, and sighs. "Well, they're all fine, Liam, but –"

"Then I'd like to discharge myself please."

"But –"

"Look, I'm nowhere near as bad as the other guys in here,
and to be honest, I'm scared about catching Covid. I'll go
to the doctors tomorrow, or whatever, so they can keep an
eye on me, but you guys are really busy, and I expect
there's someone waiting for my bed –"

"Okay. If you're mind's made up, then we can't keep you
here." She's sorted out her trolley and pushes it to the side.
"I'll just finish everyone's obs, and then I'll get your
paperwork." She smiles.

"Thanks, Ellie."

It's almost dark when I step out of the automatic doors
of the hospital and into the cold air, and the shock of it
triggers another headache. The H bus approaches, and it
hits me that I don't know how I'm going to get home. Or if
I'm even going home. I really haven't thought this through.
Dad said he'd pick me up, but I don't want to call him. I
want to find Portia, check she's alright, and get some
answers from my Uncle Richard. I start to jog up to the bus
shelter, but then see the blue snake of nurses waiting and
realise I don't have to hurry. I thought they weren't
supposed to wear their uniforms outside the hospital. But
then if the germs are on them, changing clothes will just

transfer the virus from one set of clothes to another. People don't exist in a vacuum – there's no way we can kill *every* germ. Especially if it's in us and we're breathing. I mean, if the masks stopped *everything* coming in, then air couldn't get through and we'd all be suffocating. So really, there's no escape. I shiver.

I'm so glad I've set up Samsung Pay. It gets me onto the bus and back into Exeter city centre, and from there onto the 55 back into Eskwich. People stare at the bandage on my head, so I smile at them and raise my eyebrows as if to say *I know! I m so clumsy!* There aren't many passengers, thank goodness, and no one I know, so I just plonk myself down in a 'priority 'seat and stare at the mud splashed up the window, trying not to look at my reflection and trying not to be sick in my mask.

My plan was to use the journey to work out what I'm going to do, but it's so bloody cold with all the non-closing 'ventilation 'windows open, that I find it hard to concentrate. On autopilot I check my phone, but it's just a load of pointless social media notifications and a promotional email from the RSPB. I'd switch the bloody thing off, but a big part of me is still hoping for a message from Portia. Focus.

I know Portia's at Richard's, and I know she's okay – whatever that means. I know Dad's worried about me and would want me to go straight home and call the police; that or have a chat about my genes and DNA testing, which, frankly, I can't face. If Dad isn't my dad … No, I literally can't face that. I have to go to Richard's, confront him, and get Portia out of there. The trouble is, I know damned well that he isn't going to give me any of that for free.

Given my delicate condition, I follow the signs on the bus to the letter and remain seated until the vehicle has come to a complete stop, wondering what an incomplete stop would look like. I thank the driver and rip my mask off as soon as my feet touch the concrete.

Walking up Memorial Lane, I notice the gangs of teenagers that have replaced the mobility scooter crew, on the benches. It's like when one group knocks off, the others clock on. Except for the alchies, who are always there. Other than their shouts and raucous laughter, the town is pretty dead – a typical Saturday night in Eskwich. When I get to the top of the hill, I consider dropping into The Moon for some Dutch courage, but decide against it, turning left, past the church, the past the town hall, and over the road to Richard's.

Yellow light beams through his curtainless windows, like a torch onto the night. He's in. I step up to his door. Someone has scratched *cunt* into it, and the black paint is flaking. He ought to get that seen to before the wood starts rotting. I raise my arm to bang on the door, but I hesitate, realising it's ajar, and in that moment my phone buzzes. It's a text from a number I don't recognise. *Stop prevaricating and just come in! You re letting all the heat out!*

Portia

I hear footsteps on the stairs. My blood runs cold.

"Don't worry, Portia. It's only - "

"Hello?"

I dash out of the freaky room, along the corridor, and straight into Liam. I'm embracing him, squeezing him tight, before I process the expression on his face. His arms close around the top of my back, slowly and lightly, but he doesn't let go.

"Ahh, how very sweet! That's one for the album!"

We spring apart at Richard's voice and scan each other's eyes. Richard's phone makes its I've-just-taken-a-photo sound.

"Well, sit down, everyone! Apologies, Liam – the pizza's gone cold, but you're welcome to what's left. And help yourself to a vodka and Coke." Richard smiles widely, relaxes into the sofa, stretching his arms along the back and putting his left ankle on his right knee. I perch on the sofa opposite him, and gesture for Liam to sit down next to me. He remains standing.

"Oh, come on, Liam!" Richard pats the cushion next to him. "We all know you're not going to hit me or smash me over the head with the vodka bottle, much as we all know you'd like to. Or think you ought to. Especially in front of your girlfriend. You've suffered a head injury, too - risking another one isn't sensible. Just sit down, say what you've come here to say, and then we can all get on with our lives. I have an exciting proposal for you, actually. Even Portia, here, is interested."

The glare in Liam's eyes dies. Shaking his head, he slumps down beside me. "You okay?" he asks, deadpan.

"Yeah. You?"

Liam doesn't answer. He reaches across the table and grabs a couple of slices of pizza. He turns to me. "I thought you were doing Veganuary." I try to say everything in a look, but he won't meet my gaze for long enough.

"Who's my real dad, then?"

Richard laughs. "Does it matter? I have photos to show you and a theory to share with you. It's not going to make a difference who your real father is! You're still you, and I need your skills."

"Yes, it fucking does matter! You can only understand the present and make positive changes to the future, by understanding the past – you're a palaeontologist, for God's sake, you know that! And you said it for a reason. What the fuck do you want?!"

"You know that history is written by the people in power, don't you, Liam? Truth is, essentially, a moveable feast."

"Yes, and it's our job to uncover the truth!"

"So you don't think that it's a case of not all dark places needing light, then?"

"No! And nor do you or you wouldn't have even said anything! So what the fuck do you want?!"

"I want you to help me discover – and name - a new species. Imagine being immortalised by a fossil. Has a certain poetry to it don't you think?"

"Oh. My. God." Liam separates the phrase in disbelief. "That's what this is all about. You and your fucking megalomania!"

Richard's eyes flash with what could be hatred, or murderous intention, and when he lifts his arm, I expect him to hit the table. All he does, however, is reach for a slice of pizza and chew it, thoughtfully, all the while staring at Liam.

"I really don't understand why people have such a negative view of me. In fact, I was discussing this with Portia, earlier. It used to make me angry, but now I just find it fascinating. It's almost like they're jealous of everything I've achieved …" He trails off, smirking, and pours us all a half-and-half vodka and Coke.

"I can't drink that. I'm on pain killers," Liam snaps.

"Oh, poor you," says Richard. "Paracetamol is an underrated drug, I know, but I think a line of this would be more effective." He pulls a wrap of white powder out of his jeans pocket.

"I don't do that shit. Not after what it did to Dad."

"Ah, yes, your dear father," says Richard. "Or, 'Adam', rather." He's almost drained his glass. I sip at mine, torn between the need to keep a clear head, and the need for something to take the edge off. I glance at Liam, his bandaged head, his cut and bruised arms. We haven't talked about what happened. I have no idea what's going on. All I do know, is that this situation is going to go bang at some point.

Richard racks two thick lines of coke up on the edge of the table, and snorts one through a twenty-pound note. He jerks his head back and sniffs, squeezing his eyes shut for a moment, with a quick shake of his head. "Portia?" He leans across the table and holds the note out to me.

"No, thanks." I force a smile. If Liam hadn't been here, I would have snatched the note out of his hand.

"Oh, come now! Snorting is what pigs do, isn't it?"

"What?" Liam looks a me like he doesn't know who I am.

"Her name, Liam," Richard explains, "comes from the word Latin for 'pig', which is where we get 'pork 'from. Things change over time - as they inevitably do - some bloke writes a play, and suddenly 'Portia 'is synonymous with a strong, confident, capable woman. Which, I'm presuming, is why your parents chose your name, Portia."

"Yes."

"'How far the little candle shines his – or, rather, her – light! 'If you dig a little, you uncover the whole grubby truth. Your girlfriend's name originally meant 'pig', or 'doorway'. Both are apt."

Liam looks between us both. "Sorry, have I missed

something?"

"Clearly, Liam!" Richard is loving this. Liam's eyes are fixed on him, not me.

"What's up with your voice? You're lisping."

"Ah, yes. Your girlfriend bit my tongue, so I need painkillers, too." He gestures at the line of powder, and continues, "I got this from Stuart. You remember Stuart? Manages – in inverted commas – The Riverboat. Deals cocaine on what he thinks is the sly. Your girlfriend here owes him, he owes me, therefore Portia owes me, which means you both have to come for a little holiday to the Isle of Wight. With me."

Liam freezes for a beat, then whips his gaze round to me. "What does he mean, you bit his tongue?! What the fuck's been going on?! How many more secrets are you keeping from me?!"

Costa, Eskwich, 2021

Portia

"Of course you'll come back! Everybody comes back! Eskwich has its own gravitational pull. You can never escaaaaape!" Chelsea says the last bit like a ghost, waving her hands about, and we both laugh.

Something makes me choose that moment to tell her. I stare at the table, brush a crumb off it.

"Look, Chelse, there's something I need to talk to you about."

"Oh, God, that sounds ominous!" she says, taking a sip of coffee and placing the glass down carefully in front of her. "Shit! You're not pregnant, are you?!"

"No! Of course I'm not bloody pregnant! But I am in a bit of a mess." I lift my eyes to meet hers. She's suddenly serious.

"Okay. You can tell me anything, you know. What's up?"

Where do I start?

"You know Stuart, from the pub?"

"Yeah …"

"Well, him and Liam's dad were proper coke-heads, back in the day –"

"Yeah, I know. I think Stuart still is, to be honest."

"Yeah, he is. Anyway, me and Liam were in The Riverboat one day - it must have been a Thursday night because we were having a curry – and I was desperate for the loo, but there was like a line of people queued up in the ladies', so I nipped out and went in the disabled one, because no one ever shuts the door properly, so you don't have to keep asking for the key. Anyway, the hand-drier was broken again, so someone had put a pile of paper-towels on top of it, and when I grabbed one, this plastic bag full of coke fell out and onto the floor –"

"How did you know it was coke?"

"Well, I didn't at the time! Anyway, Liam's always going on about how doing drugs is bad for you, and how people are killed and exploited for it, and how it fucked his mum and his dad up and everything, so I picked the bag up and tipped the whole lot down the loo."

"Fucking hell, Porche! That was a bold move!"

"I know. I kind of did it on the spur of the moment. And then Stuart was coming in as I was going out, and I said something like, *did you know someone s been doing drugs in there? I found some white powder and chucked it down the loo,* and he looked daggers at me and told me to follow him outside. So we're outside, and he's all up in my face, but like whispering, going on about how he'd left it there for someone to pick upon, and I'd cost him five hundred quid, and where the fuck was he going to get another load of coke from and that, and how I shouldn't have even been in the disabled toilet anyway because I'm not disabled … I mean he was *furious*! And then he said I had to pay him back. So I went back and was going to tell Liam, but I didn't want to piss him off, and I knew he didn't have any money to chuck away, so I … Fucking hell. Chelse, I'm on OnlyFans trying to make the money to pay him back –"

"OnlyFans?! What the actual?!"

"I know. But it would have taken me fucking years to pay him back out of what I make with The Body Shop and there's no way I could have asked Mum and Dad –"

"No! I mean, what the actual fuck are you paying him back for?! He's dealing drugs in a pub! He's lucky you haven't gone to the police!"

"Yeah, but I didn't want him to get into trouble!"

"He's dealing coke in the pub! He's like the fucking manager and everything! And now you're flashing your tits all over the internet! –"

"Shh! Shut up, Chelse!" I kick her legs, under the table.

"Alright, alright! So, what does Liam think about it?"

"He doesn't know."

"You're fucking prostituting yourself on the internet, Porche. There's no way he's not going to find out!"

"How will he? You know he doesn't do all that social media crap! He maybe goes on Facebook a couple times a week, but that's it! And anyway, it's not prostitution. If people are going to pay me shedloads for a few photos, then that's their look-out. I mean, it's perfect! It doesn't cost me anything –"

"Except your dignity."

"My dignity?! It's my body! I can do what I like with it! It's literally my money-maker!"

"But doesn't it gross you out, the thought of all those strangers perving over you?"

"Not really. They don't know who I am, do they?"

"But don't you worry about one of them recognizing you and following you … "

"Bloody hell, Chelse! You're my best mate! You're supposed to back me up!"

"I'm also supposed to look out for you."

Chelsea

"But you love this house, Nan! Why are you moving?"

"Because the powers that be are making it impossible for me to afford to keep living here! I'm never voting Tory again!"

I've never seen Nan like this. She's on the verge of tears, which makes me well up, too. "Oh, love, you'll understand things a lot more when you're older. I only get half of what your grandad's pension was worth, and the state pension is a slap in the face when you consider how much the bills are going up. My gas bill's almost doubled, petrol's gone through the roof … This place is too big for me now, anyway, and I can't do as much as I could in the garden with this osteoporosis –"

"I'll come round and mow the lawn!"

"Oh, love, that's very sweet of you, but look at the size of it! It used to take your grandad the best part of an hour! And then those trees … I need to get a gardener in regularly, and I just haven't got the money there to do it! Retirement isn't all it's cracked up to be!" She smiles at her statement, but there's no amusement in her eyes.

Nan stirs our coffees, and I follow her into the front room and out through the patio doors. It feels like spring today, and we both want to be out in the sunshine. Nan plonks our mugs on the table, and we sit down. I look down the garden. It really is huge, and the rhododendron at the end has sprawled so much that it completely obscures the fence. Grass is growing in the flower beds, but I've tried to dig it up before, and the soil is basically clay – heavy and claggy when it's wet, absolutely impenetrable when it's dry. I don't know how Nan and Grandad ever got anything it grow in it. But that's retirement, I suppose. You have the time to look things up, like which plants grow best in which soil and that.

"So where are you going to move to? You are staying in Eskwich, aren't you?"

Nan smiles and lights a cigarette. "'Course I am, love! I had been thinking about a bungalow, but I don't feel ready to be a proper old person just yet! I just need something smaller, in an area where I can afford the council tax. I've been on Right Move and there are a couple of places in Farefield that I could look at, one up near Wilcombe School – which would be great because I'd be near enough for you to be able to walk over – some on the new estate behind the High School, some in Cowleymoor … there are loads of places! Don't look like that, love - it'll be fine! Anyway, how's Portia getting on? She'll be off to university in September, won't she?"

Me and Brogan – the deputy manager - are standing behind the counter in Costa, waiting for someone to come in. I've got my back up against the coffee machine, he's leaning against the sink. Apart from the usual rush from about half ten till lunchtime, it's been dead in here. Covid's made a massive difference – I don't care what anyone says. I don't think anything will ever be normal again.

"Do you think they'll ever take the Wall down, Brog?" Once we were allowed to open again, they came and put this thick Perspex sheet around the whole of the serving area to keep us safe, or the customers safe, or whatever – basically trapping us behind plastic. We call it the Wall. When the coffee machine's running, you can't hear a bloody thing. People have started taking their masks off as soon as they get through the door, because they know we're going to have to ask them to repeat their orders. I made this lady a cinnamon latte the other day instead of an oat milk tea – that's how bad it is! And what's worse is that we're not even allowed to drink messed-up orders – we have to throw them down the sink. And we're using takeaway cups because the dish washer's broken again. It's such a fucking waste. All this sustainability and responsibly sourced bollocks, and we're chucking things away worse than they did in the 80s, and spraying chemicals all over the place to kill germs that probably aren't there anyway. Or if they are, they're no different to having a bad cold. I'm sure it's just an exercise in government control. I mean, Boris was always having parties, and he didn't give a shit – even though I wasn't allowed to say goodbye to Grandad. Fucking hypocrite. Nuke the lot of them, I say.

Anyway, I'm itching to get my phone out of my back pocket and scroll through Insta while I'm just standing there doing nothing, but I really need to keep this job, and I know that even though Brogan wants to do the same – he Snap Chats his girlfriend all the time – he won't get his phone out because he's going for the next Managers 'job that comes up. So we've just been stood here, chatting crap, making the odd toastie and latte for Uber Eats, for the last couple of hours, it seems like.

"I dunno," Brogan says, tapping the Wall with his knuckles. "So, did you get vacc'd in the end?" he asks. We don't seem to be able to have a conversation that doesn't involve Covid. I don't think anyone does.

"Yeah, of course," I lie.

There are two reasons why I haven't had the jab. The first is that I refuse to be told what to do. Boris and his boys can't force me to put something into my body. It's my body, and there's not enough data about whether the vaccination is safe. Also, we can't keep getting jabbed for everything. Our bodies have to build up some immunity. And I don't think it's as bad as they're making out on the news. There's fake news flying about all over the place all the time. Yes, I believe lots of old people have died, but then lots of old people die from the 'flu every year, and that's not considered an international crisis. And these stats they give out on the news – the number of Covid deaths each day. Well, you could have died from cancer but had a positive

Covid test result, so that counts as a Covid death. It's all bollocks. I think they're trying to control us. I don't think they're injecting microchips into everyone – I think they're just trying to see how much control they've got. I imagine Boris and Dominic going *I bet you can t get them to do this that and the other,* and then the other one going *challenge accepted!* I also think that if they paid hospital staff better and treated them better, more people would want to be nurses and there wouldn't be a 'crisis in the NHS 'to start with.

The other reason I won't have the jab, is that I'm hoping I might be pregnant. It's too early to do a test yet, but if I am, they still can't say for sure that it's not going to harm my baby. I mean, they say drinking and smoking when pregnant is bad for your baby and can cause all kinds of shit, but I know loads of people who've done both throughout their pregnancies and been okay. Some of them were even doing drugs before they found out they were carrying a baby. And law of averages says it 'got to work both ways. Like nuts are good for you, but they're not if you suddenly develop an allergy to them. And some cough mixtures and stuff you're not supposed to take if you're pregnant or breast-feeding, so what's the difference? And there's that whole 'survival of the fittest thing'. My boyfriend, Declan, says he'd rather keep his freedom and take his chances with Covid than keep having to go into lockdowns every five minutes. I agree with him. You can't live your whole life in fear.

Like Portia. She's so worried that she's not achieving enough, that she could be doing 'more', whatever the fuck that means, even if it's taking a three-year course that's going to put her in debt and be no use to her or anyone else ever, just because she needs to be seen to be achieving. What's wrong with having a job that pays your bills, and enjoying your life with your family and friends, without all the self-inflicted guilt and worry? If Covid's taught us anything, it's that the best thing you can do with your life is enjoy it. It's literally not fucking rocket science.

My phone vibrates in my pocket, and I take it out on impulse.

"It's three o'clock, Brog. Am I okay to get off?"

"And that's the end of that conversation! Yeah, sure, Chelse. If you've been summoned, you've been summoned, and there's not much going on here anyway."

"Sorry, Brog. It was only Porche. See you tomorrow."

"Yeah, see ya. Wouldn't wanna be ya!" He says it to everyone, like he's out of the 80s or something, but today it stings. Who would want to be me? I walk out, staring at my phone, messaging my best mate that I'm not up for a coffee or a pint. I just want to go home, put my pyjamas on, crawl into bed and watch TV. I wish *Love Island* was on.

What I end up doing, though, is walking past my house – my parents 'house, I mean – on Coleridge Road, and going through the alleys until I wind up in the park. The school's just kicked out, and the park will be full if kids and parents in a minute. I have the urge to swing round on the bars like a Catherine Wheel, like Porche and I used to when we were kids, but I think of the little life that might be inside me. I don't want to squash it. I walk past the bars, cradling my abdomen, and I carry on through the grey streets, pushing my way through groups of mums watching scruffy kids in bright blue jumpers playing tag, and gangs of friends wearing just their polo shirts and black trousers mooching home like they're part of some secret cult. I'm going to visit Nan.

It's funny how that now we live so much closer, this is only the second time I've been round since I helped her move in. I really didn't want her to sell her house on Moorhayes and, to be honest, when she told me her reasons for even thinking about moving, I didn't actually think she'd go through with it. I didn't think things were that bad. But then all I do is give my folks some money out of my wages each month for rent – I never see the bills. I never do the 'big shop', either. I guess I don't really know much.

Pushing down emerging feelings of guilt, I finally get free of the school run and head on downhill. It's not far, and even thought I can't remember what number she is; I know she's next door to the garden with all the statues. In complete contrast with her neighbour, Nan has a lawn. I say 'lawn – 'it's more of a meadow at the moment. She's even got a tree. She said when she moved in that she was going to cut all the brambles back from it – it's drowning in them – and hang up a birdfeeder so she could watch the birds from her front room window. There's a black cat poking round in the bushes – she'll probably end up luring all the birds to their deaths. When I turn up the path, the cat sprints off into the road.

There's a loud crack, and I spin round. The cat makes a horrible sound and collapses into the middle of the road. Fuck! Someone's shot a fucking cat! I hesitate, looking round for someone to help. A bunch of mums with pushchairs and little kids running around, are coming down the hill. I can't let them see the black lump in the widening red puddle in the middle of the road, so I dash out to scoop the cat up. It's got to be dead. I hope it's dead because I don't know what to do! But if it's dead, what I'm going to do with it?! Put it in the bushes and put something on Facebook, I suppose. Fuck! Who shot it? I crouch down next to the animal, but someone else's hands are already on it. The sudden realisation that there's another person so close to me, makes me jump. "Sorry!" I say, for no reason.

The old lady's watery blue eyes meet mine. "Bloody kids with their bloody pellet guns!" she says, shrugging off her cardigan and gently moving the cat onto it. "Happens all the time round here. Sorry you had to see that, love. I'll get it away before the kiddies get here."

The woman is gone before I can get up out of the road. Nan opens the door before I can ring the bell. "Oh, God, love, what's happened?"

"This cat just got shot," I say, blankly, stepping into the hall. I follow Nan to the kitchen, where she immediately puts the kettle on. "An old lady picked it up. She says it happens all the time round here. Nan, I wish you hadn't moved!" Tears sting my eyes, and I take a sip of coffee to hide my wobbling chin.

Nan smiles. "But it doesn't happen all the time, love! Yes, the woman over the road's cat went missing the other day, but it's only been a couple of days, and it isn't neutered, so it's bound to go wandering! And I've been here a week now, and that's the first I've heard of a shooting! It's hardly The Bronx! It'll be some kids messing about –"

"Oh my God, Nan! That lady who picked the cat up – does she live next door?"

"Mrs Morrell? Yes."

"Nan! She's the cat-killer!"

Nan laughs, nearly spilling her coffee. "'Cat-killer'?! Oh, love, she's not! She used to be a vet, and now she volunteers for the RSPCA or something! That's a stupid rumour made up by kids who've got nothing better to do! I was chatting to her the other day when I put the washing out. You know, it's not changed, and I doubt it ever will."

"What's not changed?"

"When I was little, if there was a woman living on her own, everyone would say she was a witch. These days, clearly, it's 'cat-killer'. Give it a couple of months, and I'll be Jaqueline the Ripper, or a spy from somewhere in eastern Europe!"

"Nan!"

"Come on, Chelsea! She's an old lady who likes gnomes, keeps herself to herself, and lives near a school. Honestly!"

Nan's got a point. I drink my coffee and we talk about my work, my parents, and reminisce about Grandad. On the walk home, two things occur to me. Mrs Morrell's watery eyes and wrinkly face contrasted greatly with the tone of her voice. And although me and Nan chatted for a couple of hours, we never talked about *her*. Maybe women on their own *don t* count in society. Maybe I ought to tell Portia.

And then it hits me - what if it was *me* they'd been trying to shoot?!

Eskwich, 2022

Portia

Chelsea messaged me this morning, asking if I wanted to meet her in town for a coffee. I'd rather meet her in town for a pint, but it is early, and she gets staff-discount in Costa.

Through the shop window, I can see her standing in the queue already, and when I go up to her, her eyes are all bright and I can tell she really wants to talk. She gets our drinks and heads to the back of the café, to the round table in the corner. She leans towards me, and keeping her voice low, she says,

"Mrs Morrell shot a cat in the street yesterday!"

"Who the fuck is Mrs Morrell?!"

"The lady who lives next door to my nan. The one with the statues!"

I know Chelse has got mixed up, or something, but I can't stop a shiver running down my spine.

"'Mrs Morrell?!'" Do you reckon we'll be calling our neighbours Mrs This and Mrs That when we're older? If I marry Liam, will you end up calling me Mrs Brookes?!"

Chelsea laughs. "Oooh hello, Mrs Brookes! How are your varicose veins today?"

"Yeah, but you know what I mean. She must have a first name. Beryl, or something."

"Beryl?!"

"Yeah! This is my problem with getting married. It's like you become part of your husband and lose your true self." I poke the cream on my hot chocolate about, searching for stray marshmallows.

"Don't be such a bloody hippy, Porche! And anyway, loads of women get married and keep their maiden names now. It's not 1894, or even 1984!" Chelsea is still laughing.

"Hmm."

"Oh. Hang on a minute! Is there something you're not

telling me?" Chelsea has pushed her latte out of the way and is leaning over the table so she's right in my face.

"What? No! No, Liam hasn't proposed, or done anything ridiculous like that." Then, under my breath, I add "Chance would be a fine thing." I kind of hope Chelse has heard me, but she's away with the fairies again.

"Do you think it's worth me calling the RSPCA, just in case?"

"What?"

"About Mrs Morrell. Oh, don't look at me like that! She's fucking dodgy, I know it!"

We fall silent for a bit. Even though Chelsea says it's dead in here most of the time, there's a new barista. He's very young, and has the loudest voice known to man. You can hear him over the coffee machine. And if he tells anyone else that they'll have to have their drinks in takeaway cups because the dishwasher is broken, I'll shove that jar of marshmallows up his arse.

I jolt up in bed, suddenly wide awake. My phone tells me it's almost two in the morning. I've been hit by the memory of a conversation I had with Liam, when he'd just come back from uni, and we were up on the canal by the footbridge. His dad had interrupted us – Liam had never told me what he saw through the letterbox of the old lady's house.

On impulse, I call Liam. His phone rings but he doesn't pick up. Maybe he's asleep. Maybe he's in a club. Maybe he's with that Georgia. Anger consumes me, even though I'm aware it's ridiculous to be angry at something that probably isn't happening, and I check to see if he's got an account with Instagram, Twitter, or TikTok and not mentioned it to me. I know he only occasionally does Facebook, but he has this whole other life I'm not part of now – he could be doing anything. When my searches draw a blank, I decide he's set up accounts in another name. I search 'Bony 99 'and variations of it, then I give up, and check his Facebook profile.

Did my anger make this happen? Did I kind of will it into being? Is it true that you reap what you sow? Or is this the thinking of someone who wishes they had that kind of power? Any power. He's been tagged in some photos *with Atlantis Georgia and three others.* He's in a club – or at least he was half an hour ago – which is packed, and the darkness is cut by coloured strobe lighting. He's in a group of people, mostly girls, and everyone has their arms around everyone else and is smiling manically. Some of them are holding shots. Liam isn't. I wonder what he's on.

Crying my eyes out, I ring his number again and again.

My phone's ringing. In that weird state between sleep and waking, I fumble under my pillow and on my duvet until I find it. It's Liam calling. I roll onto my back and consider just letting it ring off.

"Hello?"

"Portia? Are you okay?"

"Yeah. Why?"

"I've got like a thousand missed calls from you!"

I'm awake now, pull myself and a pillow up against the headboard. How sad am I?! Maybe Liam's dad was right when he said we should have split up when Liam went to Liverpool. Maybe Liam's telling the truth when he says he loves me. Maybe I'm the one causing all the chaos, because of some deep, dark hole I've got in myself. I'm lucky: I have a family, a home, income and plans. Where's all this hate come from?

"I'm sorry, Lee. I didn't think a long-distance relationship would be this hard. I think my head's fucked from all this staying in. I love you." I can hear him smiling at the other end of the phone.

"I love you, too, Porche. It's just that sometimes … ugh! …I don't know. Look, forget it. We're okay, okay?"

"Okay. Listen, this is a bit random, but Chelse's Nan has moved next door to the lady on Lazenby Road. You know, the one with all the statues in her garden. Chelse thinks she shot a cat. What did you see through her letterbox that time?"

Eskwich, 2013

Liam

I don't want to be the sort of person who lives in a box, watching the box, waiting for a box. Dad said there was no need for me to get a paper-round, but I went down to the shop on the corner of Halsbury Road and applied anyway. I say 'applied', but it was more like I went down, said I'd seen the advert in the paper, said I'd do it, and Mrs Whoever behind the counter said, *yeah, okay.*

I enjoyed doing it. Some of my friends were like, *why would you actually choose to get up before six in the morning? Fuck that!* But I'd always been an early riser, and I liked cycling through the streets when they were quiet. In winter, I'd often get halfway round before the birds started singing. And I liked the money. It felt good, this little slice of independence, the fact that if Dad was having a bad day, or was busy with Grumfer or something, and we ran out of milk, I could just nip down the shop and pick some up.

My route covered pretty much all of the Wilcombe and Tidcombe areas, and it was mainly just old people who ordered their newspapers because they'd always had their papers delivered, even though they could get the news off the telly and the internet. But then some people prefer reading paperback books to ebooks. Each to their own, I suppose. And it meant I got paid, plus tips at Christmas. And it was good exercise. Anyway, one of the houses I had to deliver to was the one on Lazenby Road that had all the statues in the garden.

There was a rumour going round at school that the lady who lived there was secretly killing everyone's cats, burying them in her garden, and putting statues over where she'd buried the bodies. When I was younger, I believed it, but now I just think she's an old lady living on her own, and someone's made up a story about her. Like the guy who used to walk past the playground every day at breaktime –

people said he was a paedo, but really, he just worked the night shift at Poultry Packers, and was walking home from the bus stop. Dad told me that one day when he picked me up, but some of the girls at school were talking about how frightened they were that if they walked home on their own, he'd get them. And mud sticks; especially in Eskwich, poor bloke.

The paper-round was part of my weekday routine for a couple of years, and I enjoyed getting my wage and my tips. Even the lady in the house with the statues gave me a tip at Christmas and Easter. She'd open the door and stand on the step, like all my other customers did – I could see down her hall and into her kitchen, and it was just a normal house; she was just a normal old lady. Until the day I had to look through her letterbox.

It was winter, and a force twelve-thousand gale was blowing. I'd had to stand up to pedal my bike up the hill, and when I got to her house I was slightly out of breath. She wasn't waiting for me, but that had been happening more and more recently. I figured she was an old lady, and her age was obviously catching up with her. I leant my bike up against her garden gate, swung the orange bag the papers were in round to my front, selected hers – *The Daily Mail* – and made my way up the garden path. I'd got into the slightly morbid habit of saying *good morning* to all the freaky statues; it was kind of a superstitious thing, like some people do when they see a lone magpie. Yes, magpies are alive, and they can actually see you – not that they're bothered in the slightest – but walking up that path in the quiet, with just the glow of the streetlights to light the way, it felt like going up the aisle of a church with the eyes of the dead congregation on you. And, yeah, I was a scientist even then, but it didn't mean I was totally closed off to the idea that there could be other kinds of energies at work in the world. After all, if energy cannot be created or destroyed, it makes sense that spiritual energy can't either.

Ugh. It's all a head-fuck. That's why I've ended up digging up fossils, and Portia's ended up digging up a different kind of dirt in books and ancient texts. That's why people go to university, isn't it, to find the answers?

I knew something was wrong before I heard the shouting. There was a kind of stifled scream, which I would have passed off as a fox if it hadn't been emanating from the house. I couldn't decide whether to bang on the door and check if the lady was alright, or just run away. But then I had her paper – I had to deliver it. Opening the letterbox was easy. It was one of those old-fashioned doors from 1970s council houses, so it was just a metal flap over a slot; no rubber and fuzzy black brushes behind it, that you have to try to shove letters through. And that's when I realised it was the lady who was shouting.

... just take your tablets and pray to God! That s all you ve got to do!

Then the voice of a girl.

You don t know what it s like! I can t think! I m dizzy! I can hardly stay awake! And I m getting fat!

Vanity is a sin, girl! You take your tablets like the doctors said and it will stop all this!

No, it won t! All the tablets do is dumb me down – they don t sort anything out!

You have a chemical imbalance in your brain, Lily, and it s for you to sort things out ! Just stop moaning, accept what s happened, and get over it! These things are sent to try us!

Yeah, that s right – you hide behind your God! None of it was your fault, was it?! And even if you kill someone you can say sorry to your God and he ll forgive you and turn you into a fucking angel, and you can go and sit up on your fucking cloud with all the rest of your self-righteous fucking family and shake your head and tut at the rest of us who actually give a shit about each other!

I'm looking through the letter box by now, and I see the

old lady slap the girl round the face. The girl flinches but stays standing and doesn't cry. Then the old lady takes the girl by her shoulders and shakes her with a strength that surprises me. *You will take your tablets and end this, or you will be forcing me to have you shut away!* She lets go of the girl, propelling her backwards, causing her to fall. The girl is in shock and sits up where she has fallen. Then the old lady storms up to her and holds the girl's nose until she opens her mouth. The lady shoves what must be tablets into the girl's mouth and bellows *SWALLOW!* Then she hands the girl a glass of water. The girl is crying. I must have made a noise, because in that instant, the girl's eyes flick to mine. I let go of the flap of the letter box, drop the paper on the doorstep and run down the path.

Chelsea

"She's such a nice lady, Mrs Morrell," Nan is saying as we sip coffee and eat our maple and pecan twists in her garden. "We often have a cup of tea together over the garden fence, and she knows so much about plants!" I can't deny it – Nan's garden is looking lovely. Her little patch of lawn is bright green and neatly mowed, and there are colourful flowers in the pots on her patio. Not that she has a proper patio, like in her old house – we have to go out of the back door – but all her old garden furniture is there, and she keeps the back door open unless it's blowing a gale, or freezing.

"She's in the hospital league of friends. You know, she fundraises, goes round talking to patients if they don't have any visitors, and things like that. She's organised a fête to raise money for the psychiatric unit –"

"A fête? At the psychiatric unit?"

"No! Not at the unit itself - I think that's illegal! No, they're putting up some stalls in the middle of Exeter. They do it every year – in Princess Hay, I think she said – and they've got a tombola and a raffle, and they're handing out leaflets and talking to people about mental health. You know, everyone's talking about mental health these days, but there's still a stigma attached. They're looking for volunteers, actually. Would you fancy it?"

"No! I'm not standing in the centre of Exeter selling raffle tickets with a bunch of old ladies! Sorry! No offence, Nan!"

Nan is laughing. "None taken, love. But you've been through some dark times, too – it might be nice to give something back."

"What do you mean, I've been through some dark times?" I can hear the aggression in my voice and try to counteract it with a small smile.

"Oh, Chelsea, love. We all saw you getting thin, and your mother does talk to me sometimes, you know!"

This is news to me. I'm shocked. My hands shake a little when I try to sip my coffee, and I don't know where to look. I didn't think Mum had even realised.

Nan is watching me. She pulls a clean tissue out of her pocket, and hands it to me. I hadn't realised I was crying. "I love you coming round to see me, Chelsea – you know I do. But the divorce hasn't been easy for your mum. She loves your dad very much. You ought to talk to her about it all. I know she'd want you to. She said to me the other day that all she wants to do is wrap you up in a big hug and tell you things will be okay. Because they will, love. It just takes time."

Portia

I take too long to answer, so obviously, Liam isn't going to believe a word that comes out of my mouth, but what can I say?! I only bit Richard because he tried to kiss me, and afterwards he hit me, but if I tell Liam that he either won't believe it, or he'll go to thump Richard, and he'll be back in hospital, maybe dead, this time. So I do what every self-respecting girl does when she can't think what to say – I turn it back on him.

"What do you mean, I'm keeping secrets?! I tell you everything!"

"Oh, really?!" Liam's face is like thunder. I've never seen him so angry. Or so hurt. I let the tears fall. "You didn't tell me you were prossing yourself out, did you?!"

I can't speak. I stop crying. I just sit there, aghast.

" How did I know?" Liam says, like he's acting being me. "Well, no one told me, don't worry about that! No, Jay's following you on Instagram, and I bet he paid for those boots, didn't he?!"

"Who's Jay?"

"My fucking housemate, Portia. You know – the one I've lived with for two fucking years!"

Liam puts his hands to his head in exasperation, knocking is bandage. He goes white and I think he's going to throw up, so I jump up and throw my arm round with the intention of guiding him onto the sofa. He shrugs me off.

"You're so fucking wrapped up in yourself all the time!" He glares at me from where he's perched on the windowsill. "I don't want to be anywhere near you! Fuck! Can you imagine how it felt to be shown my girlfriend, sitting spread-eagled on a bed with her tits out?!"

Liam is almost in tears. I don't know what to say. Richard is laughing, still relaxed back on the sofa, scrolling through his phone.

"Wow, Portia!" he says, raising his eyebrows. "You have been a busy girl! I'm actually quite insulted that you didn't kiss me!"

"It's my fucking body – I can do what I want with it! If people are going to pay me for taking a few photos, that's up to them. It's easy money!"

"Easy indeed," chuckles Richard. "But I'd hardly call it a 'few 'photos, though. There's quite a gallery here!" He turns his phone so Liam can see the screen. Liam looks away and bites his lip.

"This is so typical of you, Liam! This is why I didn't tell you! I do my Body Shop stuff, trying out make-up and taking photos of myself, and that's fine! It's fine for your pretty girlfriend to be all over the internet making money from beauty products! But when it's my *body*, that's a massive No No! You watch sex scenes on the TV, and you buy magazines, and I've heard you talking to your mates about people! It's a typical man thing! It's okay, just *not in my backyard*! You're a hypocrite! And if you'd at least offered to pay Stuart back, I wouldn't be doing it in the first place! How the fuck was I supposed to get hold of five hundred quid?! And even Chelsea said I should have gone to the police! But you? No, I can't grass up Stuart – he's doing a public service – drugs and alcohol is how people get by, isn't it? And what would your dad do without him?!"

"You leave my fucking dad out of this!"

"Why? Because he's such a great guy? Because he's found it 'so hard 'since your mum died?"

"Whoa, whoa, whoa!" Richard jumps up. Probably because he can see where this is going to end up. Back at square one. It always comes back to Liam's mum. "Liam, Portia, just chill out. I'm going to make us all a cup of coffee, and we are going to sit down sort this out like responsible adults."

"So decrees Professor Morrell." Liam pushes himself off

the windowsill and stalks off down the hall.

"Where are you going?" The words are out of my mouth before I can stop them.

"I'm going for a fucking piss, if that's okay with *Little Miss Perfect.*"

Although he hasn't been here long, and although he's not gone far away, Liam's exit leaves a void. I sit, perched on the edge of the sofa, staring at the floor. I watch Richard's feet tap for a bit, then walk out of the room. I know where he's gone when I hear the door to the room that's always closed, open. On autopilot, I go into the kitchen, fill the kettle with water and put it on to boil. *I guess it s the woman s job to make the tea,* I mutter, *it s so ingrained that I just go and do it without being asked; and no one even bothers asking!* I have taken three clean mugs out of the cupboard and spooned coffee in each before I realise what I'm doing. This might be the only opportunity I get to escape! I blew the last one, but I'm not going to blow this!

Under the cover of the noise of the old, plastic kettle, I step out of the kitchen and glance down the hall. No one's there. I want to run for the stairs, but I go quietly into the front room, just in case. It's empty. A quick look behind me, and I'm rushing down the stairs as quickly as I can. My hand reaches for the little handle on the Yale lock, and I push it down with one hand while I push the door with the other. My heart's going like mad. The door doesn't open. I hear the toilet flush. Try again. I'm locked in! I scan the dirty hallway looking for the key to the deadlock. No key! Try again! This is madness! OPEN! My hand slips and my finger catches on a little button. Yes! I remember how these doors work! I slide the button upwards, and it clicks as I hear footsteps, some papers shuffling, Richard saying, "Fuck's sake, Liam! Does she always take this long to make a coffee?!" But I'm out! As a gesture to Liam, and to buy me a few more seconds, I leave the door open and peg it down the hill, over the bridge and crash into the double doors of The Riverboat. The pub's shut! It must be about five in the morning. Fuck!

Chelsea

Mum drops me off outside Costa, and the clock above the health-food shop chimes six. I hate these early starts in the winter – going to work in the dark just shouldn't be a thing. I turn and wave to Mum, who smiles and drives off, then I push the door. It's locked. Brogan's late again. Fucking hell – it's freezing! I stamp my feet and put my hands round my neck to try to warm them up.

"Chelsea!" My name comes out like a scream, and I snap my head in the direction of the noise.

"Portia?" My questions are knocked out of me as she slams into me, hugs me, and tries to push us both inside.

"What?!" Her eyes show terror. "Porche, what's up?! Are you okay?"

"We have to get inside! Why won't the door open?" She's almost in tears.

"Brog hasn't got here to open up yet," I tell her. She sobs and drops to the ground. "Portia!" I crouch down and put my arm round her. These trousers are getting tight. I'll have to switch to skinny lattes. Unless it's not the lattes … Then I take in the state of my best friend. "Oh my God, Porche! What's happened to you?!"

"Alright, ladies?! Is this a private party, or can anyone join in?"

Portia scrambles to her feet. "Brogan! Open the door! Open the door, please! We need to get inside!"

With a concerned frown, Brogan unlocks the door and the three of us step quickly inside. "Lock it! Lock it, quickly!" Portia urges, and he does so, before dashing over to switch the alarm off. Portia pulls me to the table behind the coffee machine, and I slump down onto the chair next to her.

"Right!" says Brogan once he's turned the lights on and fiddled about with the coffee machine, "Anyone want to tell me what's going on?"

"Porche?"

I look at my friend. "Can I have a hot chocolate first, please?"

Liam

I try doing the hand-against-the-glass thing one more time, but with the same result. It would be madness to do this again. For some reason, even though I'm a 'long-term memory', Grumfer won't accept me. It's like he's changed. Like he's gone. And if he's gone, then why would I keep putting hm through this? I quite literally could be anyone, standing up against his window. I have to get on with things. Grumfer's gone, and however much he looks like the same person, he's not. I want him to know me because we were so close when I was growing up. It hurts like *fuck* that he doesn't recognise me; that for him, I just never existed. It hurts like fuck. But I can't do this again. It's no good for either of us.

Grumfer remembers Dad, though. Dad sometimes gets a few words out of him. He always gets a smile. Much as I want to hear about how Grumfer's doing, and that he's okay – or whatever passes for 'okay 'in there – I've started dreading Dad coming back from the home and wanting to talk to me. But he has no one else to talk too so what can I do?

And then one day he comes back and tells me that Grumfer's caught Covid. That they've moved him to hospital. That he's on a ventilator. That he might not make it. That we're not allowed in to see him.

Dad pulls a couple of beers out of the fridge, and we sit on the battered sofa staring at the TV screen. Shadow stretches out between us, his front paws touching Dad's thigh, his back ones touching mine.

Dad and I don't even go out the front door the next day. Dad calls the hospital a lot, but they're busy, and in any case, there's nothing else to say. They're *doing all they can.* They'll call us *if there s any change.* I wait till eleven o'clock before I crack open my first can. Dad chain smokes.

I know we ought to get out in the fresh air, take some exercise; that sitting in like this isn't doing either of us any good. But it's easier to stay in, mooch between the fridge and the sofa, get pissed. Dad goes upstairs to bed. Portia calls and texts me a million times, but I let my phone vibrate on my leg while I watch TV. Later, I get a WhatsApp message: *I'm coming round.*

The doorbell goes. I ignore it. She looks through the windows. I get up and close the curtains. She almost screams through the letterbox, *Liam! I know you're shagging her! I know you are! Why don't you come out and talk to me like a man?!* She bangs her fists on the door. *I fucking love you!*

Eventually, it goes quiet. Eventually, Dad plonks himself back down on the sofa next to me. He's holding a can of Thatchers between his legs, twisting it round and round, staring at it. *Game of Thrones* is on, but I can't make out which episode it is, so I can't tell Dad what the hell's going on. But it doesn't matter.

"The hospital just rang," he says.

I turn my head to meet his eyes, but the rest of me is frozen.

"He's gone." There's a long silence. "Grumfer's gone. A nurse came to check on him, and he was gone. He died on his own. He died on his own and we're not allowed to go and see him, and if we're allowed a funeral, it'll just be me and you. But yeah. He's gone."

Dad shrugs, and tries to smile, but his face contorts. He turns his back on me and downs his cider. He goes to walk out of the room, but he stops in the doorway.

"D'you want another one?" he says, voice cracking. I'm about to say *yes* when there's a bang. Dad's side-on up against the kitchen wall, sobbing. "He wanted me to scatter his ashes on the Isle of Wight. How the *fuck* are we supposed to do that?!"

Richard

The kettle stops boiling and I light my cigarette. There is a distinct absence of the sound of clinking spoons in cups of coffee, so I ask my nephew – sorry, Liam – again. "Does she always take this long to make a cup of coffee?"

Liam is pacing up and down in front of the window. "It's freezing in here," he comments, pulling the sash down even though I'm smoking. The smoke continues to drift out towards the hall. I can still feel a draft. I crush my cigarette into the ashtray already knowing what's happened. The kitchen is empty.

"The front door's open," Liam calls from the top of the stairs. We stare at each other for a beat.

"Go and close it, then." I love these moments. Moments when things are slightly out of control. I think it's the adrenalin rush. Will Liam take off down the road, too? Will I run after him? Will he call the police? Has Portia got to a phone already, and they're on their way? Will I stay here and wait for them to arrest me, and then kill myself in prison? Or will I just get in my car, head east and try to make it to the Isle of Wight?

My questioning – along with the rush – is cut short because Liam has closed the door and is stomping back up the stairs. His face is a picture of hate. For that split second – and only for that split second – I feel for him. He reminds me of me. He's glaring at me.

"Tell me who my real dad is, and I'll help you."

I pat my pockets for change and my phone. I have two phones. Ah! I'd forgotten! The other one is Liam's! Liam spies his phone and makes to grab it from me, but eventually he sees sense and leaves it where I place it, on the coffee table. I find Portia's smashed one and lay it next to his. Liam cleans up a bit, while I snort the other line of coke and stuff the rest into my pocket. I grab my travel bag, along with the equipment and notes we'll need. Liam downs the rest of the Coke from Dominoes and grabs the bottle of vodka. I tell him I'll buy him toiletries and clothes when we get there, and we leave the maisonette.

"What, are we seriously going in your car?!" Liam says as I open the boot and sling my bag inside.

"Well, Liam, how else are we going to travel? Would you like to walk it? It's —" I check my phone, "about one hundred and thirty-three miles."

"So we're actually going to the Isle of Wight, then?"

"Well, yes."

"Even though Portia knows you want to go there? If she's called the police, that'll be the first place they look —"

"Liam, Liam, Liam. Think about things for a moment," I say. "And while you're thinking, get in the car. Never mind the blood — it's mine." I open the double doors, get in my car, and drive it onto Angel Hill. "Close the doors, please, Liam." While I'm idling, I consider driving off and doing this myself. No — it will be quicker with two of us. He gets back in and slams the door. "If she'd called the police, don't you think they'd be here by now?"

"Fair point."

I shove the car into first gear, and we wheel spin off up the hill.

Chelsea

I can't believe I'm even doing this. Nan offers to drive me, but I decide to get the bus into Exeter, in the hopes that it won't show up, and then I won't have to go, and it won't be my fault. It's a cop-out, I know, but it's going to be so fucking awkward making small talk with old people. I hope none of my mates see me. I mean, seriously, are tombolas even a thing still?

The bus arrives. It's a double-decker, so once I've got my ticket, I head upstairs and sit right at the front. I'm lucky – I'm the only one up here. I put my feet up on the windowsill, put my earphones in and watch the white lines in the middle of the road as they snake through the green of the Exe Valley. I used to do this journey a lot, but today I find myself flinching every time the top of the bus whacks an over-hanging branch.

When I get off, I head straight down the path that runs behind Next – I'm going to go the backway in and do a bit of a reckie. I have Mrs Morrell's number – I can always call and say I got on the wrong bus, or I'm feeling sick, or something. Actually, no, I can't – Nan would see right through it and then she'd be upset because of me, and I don't think I could handle that. I have to go through with it. Ugh. To bolster my spirits, I decide to pop into Coffee#1, but when I arrive, the queue is so long I don't even bother going in. I turn right and walk under the sort of cloister bit, past Coal and Costa, and up to gazebos I can see lining the road at the top.

I'm surprised by the crowd that's gathered in front of them. I spot Mrs Morrell, a couple other old ladies and a lad who's not much older than me. Each one of them is deep in conversation with a passer-by, so I kind of loiter at the back until Mrs Morrell's person signs up for a monthly donation and walks away.

"Umm, hi, Mrs Morrell. I'm Chelsea." She turns her watery blue eyes on me and smiles.

"Ah, yes, hello! Glad you could join us – it seems as though it's going to be a busy morning! And call me Joyce today, love, please."

Joyce (not Beryl – I'll have to tell Porche) introduces me to the others. The lad is called Jack, and he's actually been in the psychiatric unit. It's called The Beeches. He tells me that Mrs Morrell's daughter was in there at the same time as him. I didn't realise Mrs Morrell even had a daughter.

Within half an hour, I'm enjoying myself. Mrs Morrell – I can't get used to calling her Joyce - has put me in charge of the tombola, and I can't believe how many people are coming over and buying tickets! The prizes are eclectic though – everything from bubble bath to free tickets to the football to a creepy stuffed seagull in a glass display case.

"I feel sorry for the poor fucker who wins that!" I say to Jack, and he laughs and tells me that it *takes all sorts,* and I feel embarrassed for being judgemental. After all, Mum collects clowns, and I know that wasn't the reason Dad left.

"Okay, folks, I think we should give it another twenty minutes and then pack up," Joyce announces. The time has flown, but she's right – it'll be dimpsy soon, and now I think about it, I'm pretty cold. Jack does one last Costa-run, and Joyce and I start collecting all the leaflets together, binding them into piles with elastic bands.

"Hi."

I jump and look round. "Can I have a go on the tombola before you pack up, please?"

"Uh, yeah, sure," I say to the guy in front of me. He must be in his fifties, but he's still quite fit, and there's not much grey peppering his black hair. He hands me 50p, and I turn the handle on the tombola while he stares at me so hard that I blush and have to look away.

I slide back the door and let him pick a ticket. His hands

are thick and strong and coarse. I bet he lifts weights.

"I've got green forty-two," he says, flipping the ticket round to prove he's not cheating. I scan the prizes. Oh my God.

"Oh, I'm so sorry! You've won the stuffed seagull! Do you want to pick another ticket for free?"

The man laughs. "Don't be silly – it's perfect! This is for charity, and my girlfriend was unfortunate enough to have had to spend some time in The Beeches. Someone's donated something they spent a long time making. Taxidermy is a skill, you know, and I kind of like the look of the old fellow. I'll take what I've won, please!"

I smile, thank him, and hand him the dead bird in the glass coffin. I'm sure it's looking at me.

"Thanks," he says as he turns to go. "Oh, and by the way, the correct term for this species of bird is 'gull'," he says. "There's no such thing as a 'seagull'."

Liam

I pulled a knife on Stuart. I didn't really mean to, and it was only my string-knife, but the fact remains that to on-lookers, that's what happened. I was lucky I didn't get barred. Or arrested. I looked it up – what I did is called *affray*. And I fucked up my first impression with Professor Morrell! I mean what are the chances of meeting an expert palaeontologist – the one I'm hoping will be teaching me when I get to uni in the autumn – in a shitty Wetherspoons in Eskwich?! And how on earth is Stuart his friend?! I guess it just goes to show that you can't judge a person by what you see on the internet. But then we all have lives, don't we? I mean, yes, he's a professor, but he had to be born somewhere, and he's bound to go to the pub sometimes – you can't spend your whole life on a dig or studying: God knows, I've tried. Of course he has friends who aren't academics! I just never expected in a million years that a person like Stuart would be one of them!

And how did he know my dad's cat died?! How does he know my dad? As I walk slowly back through town, I Google him on my phone. All I can find is his PhD thesis and his university profile. He doesn't do Facebook, unless he uses a fake name, but I don't think that's his style. He has a Twitter account, but it's only a few years old. He doesn't Tweet often, and when he does, it's only professional stuff. I try Instagram. He's there, but it says the account is private. I don't even bother with TikTok.

I'm at Loman Green before I put my phone away. There's a seagull sitting on Edward the Peacemaker's head, as usual. I walk down the sloping path, then onto the grass verge. I sit with my back against the old horse chestnut tree and watch the colliding currents in the shallow water. I've only been there about twenty seconds when the first load of ducks come gliding out from under the bridge like it's a waterslide. They're all female, all mallards, all gobby as fuck.

"I don't have any food for you, guys!" I tell them, before glancing around to make sure no one's heard me talking to a bunch of ducks. They're totally unafraid and come right up to me, quacking really loudly. Some males join them – even the one with the gammy leg. I remember the first time I saw that duck. It was a couple of years ago, and I got straight onto the phone to the vets because I was so worried about it. They said if I could catch it, I could bring it in and they'd take a look at it, but as there was nothing wrong with his wings and seemed to be able to swim quite well, I had no chance of getting hold of him. I called some animal rescue places, but they were busy as fuck and asked me what condition the duck was in. It was fat, like all the others; its feathers were shiny; apart from a bit of a limp, it seemed to be able to get about just fine. They said there was no point sending someone down because it might not be there when they arrived, and they just didn't have the manpower anymore. If it looked healthy, it was probably fine. They told me to keep an eye on it and to let them know if I thought it was suffering, and that if I managed to catch it, I could take it to a vet and go from there; I should bear in mind that all that would be very stressful for the duck, though.

I'd never thought of it like that. I guess it's because if you see a person in trouble, you try to help them, and they can get sorted for free on the NHS. But you can't explain to a wild animal that you're just trying to help it, and I know that cats and dogs can get about fine on three legs, or with one eye. And of course they didn't have enough staff or vehicles or time or money to spend a day trying to catch every single wild animal that wasn't physically perfect. I thought of all the rancid pigeons in Trafalgar Square when Dad used to take me up to London at Christmas when I was little. And where do you stop? How many crushed worms had I seen in my life on the pavements? Some of my school friends used to set fire to ants with magnifying glasses in the summer. One kid used to catch daddy longlegs and pull the wings and legs off. People used to laugh. Cunts.

Anyway, I kept an eye on the duck, making a point of going for a walk down to Loman Green every day, and sitting there for a bit to see if he'd turn up, every time I was in town. One day I was sat there under the tree, and this bloke in a high-vis jacket came down with a big bag of bird seed and started chucking it about everywhere.

"Nice spot," he said to me.

"Yeah," I said, vaguely, watching the ducks as they appeared from nowhere to get the seed. The duck with the gammy leg arrived, dragging himself out of the fast-flowing water. A thought occurred to me. "Mate, do you come here often?"

The guy laughed, and then so did I because it hadn't meant to come out like a chat-up line. "No, I mean, do you feed the ducks here a lot? It's just you're in a Mid Devon Council jacket … I was thinking this might be part of your job …?"

The man laughed again. "Nah, mate, this isn't my job! I get to empty the bins and pull the shopping trolleys out of the river, and stuff. Nah, I just get a bag of duck food from the pet shop and come down here on my breaks."

"I didn't know they did duck food at the pet shop."

"Are you in the pet shop much?"

"No."

"Then how would you know? Don't worry about it, mate. I just think it does them some good to get some proper food instead of bits of sandwiches and sausage rolls all the time. That shit's bad for them, and it makes them disinclined to find their natural food. Killing with kindness, really."

"Yeah, I suppose so. Mate, what I was going to ask you was, have you seen that duck with the gammy leg before?" I point to the duck. He's over on the grass on the other side of the path, quacking like fuck. I guess he doesn't want to get missed.

"The Doctor, you mean?" He points to the duck with the gammy leg.

"Yeah. Sorry, why do you call him The Doctor?"

"Because he quacks."

I can't help but laugh. The man's nearly out of duck food now. "Sorry, mate, I'm just interested because I tried to get him to the vets once – how long's he been like that? And do you reckon he's suffering?" I'm going to have to move in a minute – the sun's gone round and I'm now sitting in shadow. The grass is cold and now feels wet under my bum.

"Oh, that's very kind of you, but you're not the first, and you won't be the last! Nah, The Doctor's been here since I-don't-know-when. He gets about okay, and he doesn't look like he's starving, does he?! He got shot by a pellet gun, although no one saw who did it – probably some bored teenagers, you know what they're like. No offence, mate!"

"None taken! So what happened?"

The man shakes the remaining seeds out of the plastic bag, screws it up and chucks it in the bin. "Some old duck – haha! See what I did there?! – yeah, some old duck who's a retired vet saw him, got hold of him and checked him over, apparently. He was doing okay, so she left him to it. I just make sure I give him an extra handful or two of food when I see him! Right, I've got to get on, mate. See ya!"

"Yeah – see ya," I murmur, but he's already back on Gold Street, heading into town.

Chelsea

Once we're packed up, I don't know whether to hang around and go back with everyone else, or whether I'm supposed to just say 'bye 'and catch the next bus, so I just stand around looking awkward until Jack comes over and asks if I'd like to get a coffee.

I'm glad when he suggests Coffee#1- it's my favourite coffee shop in Exeter, but when we get there, I realise I'm all coffeed out. We're in the queue, looking at the cakes behind the glass, and Jack asks me what I want. I dither, and he smiles, saying, "You know what? I think I've had enough coffee today. Shall we go for a pint instead?"

Retracing our steps, we end up in The Ship. We go there because I've always wanted to go in there. It's just the look of the place. It's in up a little alley that runs from Cathedral Green to the city centre, so it's always dark, especially since The Royal Clarence burnt down and they put up all the scaffolding and temporary construction walls. From the outside, it looks like it was transported from Shakespearean times – all Tudor wood panelling, and stained-glass windows, with a rickety old wooden sign with a pirate ship on it, blowing like crazy in the wind-tunnel of the alley. Jack pushes open the greying, creaking wooden door and we step onto a pine-effect laminate floor to the sound of Rhianna's *Hey DJ.*

Jack looks at me, and we both crack up! We walk past round, modern tables with smooth wood-effect chairs that have probably come straight out of Ikea and lean up against the bar. Jack orders a San Miguel, and I order a Corona, which comes with a chunk of lime stuck in the top of the bottle. We find a table near the windows and sit down.

"I'm so glad you didn't make the joke," Jack says, taking a massive gulp of his beer.

"What joke?"

"'I'll have a Corona, please, but hold the virus.'"

"F- seriously, do people actually say that?"

"Yep. I work in The Imperial – I get it a lot."

"Wow."

"Yeah," he says, raising his eyebrows.

"So," I begin, completely forgetting how to start a normal conversation, "you've been in The Beeches?"

"Yeah. I'm bipolar. Had a bit of a breakdown."

"Must have been one hell of a breakdown if you ended up sectioned."

"Yeah."

"Fuck. I'm sorry. I don't mind if you don't want to talk about it!"

Jack laughs. "Well, I've kind of been talking about it all day! Just trying to prove that mental illness is the same as physical illness … you know, 'just because I've been detained under a section of the Mental Health Act, it doesn't mean I'm going to come round and kill your dog', type of thing."

I laugh again. "Do you know what, Jack? I've felt like such a fraud all day. I've never been sectioned … I was only on anti-depressants for a few months …"

"Yeah, but that doesn't mean there was nothing wrong! It's not like Top Trumps, you know!"

I just smile. "Well, we raised a load of money, anyway."

"Yeah. We always do. And we had some good prizes."

I nearly sneeze lager out of my nose. "Yeah, but what about that stuffed seagull?! Oh my God, I was so embarrassed when that guy won it! I told him he could have another go, but he just took it! He seemed to like it!"

"Yeah, well, it takes all sorts, doesn't it?"

"Yeah, but a stuffed seagull in a jar?! I swear it was staring at me the whole time!"

"Yeah, I admit it – they're weird, but don't let Joyce hear you say that!"

"Why not?" My Corona is almost empty already and I'm

having fun. I think I'm going to text Mum and tell her I won't be back till late.

"Because she makes them."

This time I really do spit beer all over the table, and some of it goes on Jack. "Nice," he says, "thanks for that!" He's laughing, but I'm mortified. And not just because I spat my drink over someone I quite fancy. And I've just realised what an unconsciously good choice of word 'mortified 'is.

"Seriously? She makes them?" Something about his expression tells me that I don't have to worry about being laughed at for being gullible.

"Yeah. No! not like that! Not as raffle prizes! Oh my God, no! No, she makes them for museums and that. She used to be a vet … I know, it's really weird … but she only makes them for natural history displays … she does it for free … and she only uses roadkill. You know, and things that are already dead. She does a lot of work for charity …"

"Hang the fuck on! 'She does a lot of work for charity'?! So that's okay, then?! She kills animals and takes all their innards out and stuffs them with whatever the hell you stuff them with, and that's okay?! Oh my God, I think I'm going to be sick!"

I'm aware that I've shouted, and that people are looking at us. I'm aware that Jack is now mortified. He's saying something, but I'm so blown away that I'm not processing his words. I have to get out of this place as fast as possible and phone the police. Oh my God! The rumours were true. They were fucking true!

I'm standing up and have left the table and am out of the door and back on the main high street before Jack catches me up.

"Chelsea! Will you just listen!" He's caught me by the arm and spun me round so I'm facing him again. "This is the typical reaction people have! To be honest, I was kind of hoping you were better than that –"

"She kills people's cats! She doesn't use just roadkill; she kills people's pets!" Jack is staring at me in disbelief. "Jack! This has been going on for *years*! My nan lives next door to her – that's how I came to be doing this thing today – and rumours have been flying round about her since I was a little kid!"

Jack is suddenly calm. He walks me over to the nearest metal bench and sits me down. "Chelsea. You *met* Joyce. You *saw* her working today. She does all this – and much more – out of the goodness of her heart. And she does it because she lost her daughter." He pulls a pouch of tobacco out of his pocket. I didn't know he smoked. Maybe that's why he was always the one offering to go and get us coffees. He rolls a cigarette, and gestures to ask me if I'd like one. I shake my head.

"I was in The Beeches with Lily – I told you that. She was *really* ill. Her diagnosis was bipolar disorder, but ... I don't know ... I think she had a lot of other stuff going on too. We kind of got on while we were in there together ... I could talk to her without feeling awkward or on guard, you know? Anyway, she told me that she'd been in and out of places like that all her life – she'd be ill and go in, and then she'd be okay for a bit, get out, get a job and that, and then something in her would just crash and her mum would have to get the doctors in, and she ended back inside. And if it was hard for her, it must have nearly killed her mum. So Joyce got involved in fundraising. And, like, raising awareness and that. That's why she does all this."

"What had happened, to make her so ill? Lily, I mean."

"I dunno. She never said. She said she was bored with talking about it, so she'd tell me about the birds that were singing, or about music and that. Joyce said that the doctors put it down to a chemical imbalance in her brain. You know, like some people get diabetes and that. And then when Lily died, Joyce just went all out with the charity stuff, trying to get people to talk about their mental health. The 'It's okay to not be okay 'thing –"

"Oh. That crock of shit. Of course it's not okay to not be okay! That's the whole fucking point!" I want to add *and another thing that s not okay is taxidermy!* But I don't.

"Really? Do you think so?" Jack looks at me in a deep kind of way that kind of suggests pity. "So you had anorexia. How did you get through that?" It's a challenge more than a question from someone who's interested. He seems angry.

"Well, I took anti-depressants for a bit, did a bit of therapy, got over it, I suppose." I check myself. "No, I don't think I've got over it. I think I just manage things better."

"Exactly. You spoke to someone and you felt better. Someone's got to train those people, you know. And for all its slogans and soundbites, the government isn't exactly flooding Mental Health with cash, you know. People like Joyce do that."

"And people like you."

"And you."

I watch people coming out of Tesco with bags-for-life full of shopping. I watch the hoodies-and-tracksuit gangs that gather between the pillars, smoking. I watch the homeless couple drag their sleeping bags further around themselves. They can't be much older than me. The bloke is holding a can of Tesco cider, taking the odd swig and passing it to his girlfriend. They're not even begging. They're just sitting there. My first thought is that they're on drugs and their parents have kicked them out. I guess that's what most people think, and that's why they're passing them by, avoiding looking at them. But they know they're there. What is it about humans and burying their heads in the sand?!

"So why do you really think Joyce is an animal murderer? Is it because a bunch of kids in your class said she was?"

Keeping my eyes fixed on the homeless couple, I reply, "It was at first. Then I didn't believe it. But then Nan moved next door … and then I saw this cat get shot, and Joyce was the first person there …"

"But she was a vet before she retired."

"I know, but she has all these statues in her garden."

"So?"

"So, it's *weird*!"

"What, just because you don't like them?"

"*No*! God, Jack! Look, you're trying to prove me wrong, but how do you know you're right?"

"Because I was in hospital with Lily."

"Who was ill."

"Yes."

"And you don't think that maybe she could have been ill because her mum was such a freak?!"

"Oh my God, Chelsea! Look, I don't know what to believe most of the time! No one really knows the truth about anyone, do they? And it's our actions that make us what we are, and Joyce does shed loads for charity. Out of the goodness of her heart. For nothing. She's a good person. And I think you're the one with the issues if you think she's a pet-killer. Fuck's sake. Look, my bus is just coming up the road, and I think I'm going to get on it. I think you should probably go home too."

"Jack –"

"Thanks for your help today, Chelsea." And he's gone.

Richard

Part of me is disappointed that Portia didn't call the police – I could have done with a chase. What a strange girl! I wonder why she didn't. I take the M5 at a steady eighty miles an hour, and then it's onto the 303 for miles and miles and miles.

Liam and I drive in silence. I tried putting some music on but found I couldn't concentrate. Probably the lack of sleep and the volume of alcohol in my blood. Also, my tongue is doing my head in. It's fat and raw, and eating is painful. Coffee's not going down well, either, which is an issue. All I can comfortably consume is cold water. I'm a bit dizzy and I certainly don't want to be pulled over. I slow to sixty and push my anger down when the road becomes one lane – I daren't overtake.

From time to time I glance over at Liam. He doesn't look well. His twitching chin suggests he's perpetually on the verge of tears, and he stares down the middle of the road. Weirdly, I'm finding the silence oppressive.

"How long have you been with the delectable Portia, then?" I ask. Ugh. What a vacuous thing to say.

Silence. "I said, how long have you and the delectable Portia been together?"

"Fuck off, Richard."

Great! A spark. I am immediately in better spirits. Smiling, I let his hatred or anger or whatever it is, fill the car until it's almost tangible. We're approaching Stonehenge.

"Pull over."

"I beg your pardon?"

"Pull over. In the car park. At Stonehenge."

I'm not usually one to obey orders, but this seems interesting. I gleefully flick my indicator on, and we turn off the A road. I snake my car along to the carpark, and as soon as I've cut the engine, Liam pops his seatbelt and jumps out.

Carefully and deliberately, I do the same. Liam is staring off in the direction of the stones, breathing deeply like he's psyching himself up for something. Is he thinking about running? I take a deep breath too. And then the nausea overwhelms me, and I run over to the hedge and throw up. When I'm empty, I stand there, head down with my hands on my knees, spitting.

"Are you okay?"

"What the fuck do you think?!" I feel too rough for sarcasm. Liam hands me a bottle of water. "Where did you get that?"

"From the shop." He points to a low building. A tourist centre.

"Thanks." I walk back to the car, find the ibuprofen I always keep in the side of the door, and swallow three caplets.

"You're only supposed to take two every four hours!"

"Fucking hell, Liam. I've been drinking vodka and snorting cocaine all night!"

"Fair point."

"So, what are we doing here, anyway? Is this some jolly uncle-nephew bonding exercise?"

"I want to walk around the stones. Also, I think we should eat something."

I wish I'd come here in the 60s or 70s when you could actually touch the stones. Things are so antiseptic these days – and not just because there's a hand-gel station every three metres. They've given us headphones so we can listen to a documentary, and we follow a load of tourists slowly around the perimeter. Liam wears his headphones like a scarf, and I do the same, even though I'd love to hear the commentary. Some of the tourists have proper cameras and take time lining up their shots even though it's a grey day, so all they'll get is a dark grey silhouette against a pale grey sky. The rest of them click away on their phones.

I'm torn. I want to ask Liam what he's getting from this, but I can't separate myself from the power of the mystery of the stones. I can feel the weight of history trying to touch me and realise I have stretched out my arm. I try to imagine this place full of hippies on Midsummer's Day, or the summer solstice, whatever it's called. Kayleigh would have loved this. I'm slightly aroused, thinking about fucking her on one of the low stones, then slitting her throat and sacrificing her to all the gods; to any gods. I can see her blood trickling down the rock and pooling a little on the grass it stands on. I imagine lapping it up, while she sprawls there all open and glorious, and then fucking her again once her heart's stopped. And then I remember that's she's already dead, that someone's already stabbed her, and that her arterial blood soaked the tarmac on Dryden Road. What a violent way to go for such a lovely person! She deserved better. She deserved some weird, spiritual drama. She deserved to be offered up to her goddess on stones laid by her ancestors, her cadaver wrapped in purple velvet and commended to the earth in a shallow grave nearby, an oak sapling for a headstone. She would have loved that. She would have loved it here. I wonder if she ever visited.

The urge to put on the headphones and glean some information and history from the experts overwhelms me, and I'm just settling them over my ears when Liam says, "I come here with my dad every year on the day before the summer solstice. For Mum."

The statement hits me like a blow to the temple.

"Except Adam isn't my real dad, is he?" I stay silent. "I mean, he is my real dad in the sense that he's the one who brought me up, but he's not my biological dad, is he? I can feel it. I've always felt like something didn't quite fit, and now I know what it is. You're my real dad, aren't you?"

I can hear his tears emerge as he ends the sentence. I actually do feel for him.

"That's why I couldn't tell the police that you knocked me out and left me for dead. Some fucked up biological impulse. That's why I couldn't run after Portia. That's why I've always been so focussed. It's why I love dinosaurs –"

I can't supress my laughter at this. "You can't inherit a love of dinosaurs and a passion for history! That's like saying you've inherited a fear of heights!"

"Don't fucking laugh at me, *Dad*!"

"Don't fucking call me 'Dad', *Will*iam! I'm no more your dad than I am your uncle! God! Me?! A father?! No fucking chance – I'm way too sensible for that!"

"Sensible?! You raped my mum! And my name is Liam, not fucking William!"

"You do realise that your mother named you after Liam Gallagher, don't you, Liam? The name on his birth certificate is *William* Gallagher, and that *Liam* is a nickname he's chosen to use? In the same way that *Will* is?" I pause to give him time to process this information, but for an intelligent kid, he's thick as pig-shit. I sigh and continue. "I did have sex with your mother, and when she finally informed the police that I *hadn t* in fact killed her best friend, she dropped all charges. I am innocent."

"Yeah. But only in the eyes of the law."

"Truth is a moveable feast, depending on who's eyes you're looking through."

"You're a fucking bastard."

I weigh up the sentence. "No. I'm a survivor. And I am definitely *not* your father."

"Then who is?"

"We're nearly back at the start. I'm going to ask them if we can walk round once more, with our headphones on. I'll say we were trying to absorb the vibes, or something."

Eskwich, January 2022

Portia

"You have to call the police, Porche!"

"I know, but I can't. I know this sounds fucked up, but I really want him and Liam to discover a new species. Then it'll be over. Richard can't be looking for me – he would have found me by now. It's not like there are many places in Eskwich open at this time in the morning! And Liam knows you work here!"

Brogan interrupts. "Look. Whatever you decide to do, I've got to open up in a minute, and Chelse, I need you to work. Portia, go home and clean up and then when you've decided what you're going to do, text Chelse and we'll go from there. You can't just sit here – you look a state, and you stink of … well, you just generally stink, actually. No offence."

I drain my now not-so-hot hot chocolate. It's made me feel better. Stronger. "I can't. Richard smashed my phone." Chelsea gasps and spits out a run of expletives. Brogan says,

"Well, pick up a pay-as-you-go from Tesco or something. But Chelse's right – you should go to the police. I mean, this Richard's nearly killed your boyfriend already; fuck knows what he's doing to him now."

"Yeah, cheers for that, Brog," Chelsea says. She gives me another hug, then stands and picks up my cup. There's a line of customers outside the door. The guy at the front knocks on the glass as I catch his eye. I need to be strong.

"Right. Thanks, Chelse; thanks, Brogan. I'm gonna go and let you get on before your regulars start bashing down the door. I'll pick up a phone on my way home. Can you write your number down, Chelse?"

Chelsea laughs, eyebrows raised. "Seriously, I've been your best friend forever, and you still don't know my number?!" I must have looked ashamed, because she gets a serviette, grabs a pen from behind the counter, and scrawls her number on it.

"Oi! Are you lot going to open up today, or what? Some of us have got to get to work!" It's the guy in the front of the queue.

"Okay, I'm going!" I say, and follow Brogan to the door. The guy barges in before I can get out.

"Family crisis," Brogan calls to the man. "Apologies."

The man looks a bit sheepish when he clocks the state of me, but he says nothing.

"Good luck!" Chelsea shouts from behind the plastic Covid wall. I smile and step out into the cold.

I am actually ashamed that I don't know Chelse's number off by heart, but then she did go through a phase of losing her phone on a night out and getting a new one with a new number. But what does it mean that I have Liam's number tattooed on the inside of my eyelids? It means I love him. I'm pretty sure he's shagged this Atlantis, but when he's told me he loves me, I do feel it. I pop into Tesco to get a new phone, only to find that the phone bit doesn't open until ten. Fuck. I'll have to go home.

"Portia? Is that you?"

"Yeah. Sorry, Mum!" I actually go over and hug her. I don't think I've done that since I was a kid.

"Oh, love, are you okay?" she says into my hair. "Me and your dad have been worried!"

"I know. I'm sorry. Is Dad still here?"

"No, he had to head off to work early. He's in Plymouth today." She pauses, breaks out of the hug, and walks into the kitchen. I follow. "So are you going to tell me where you've been all night?"

While the kettle boils, I tell her Liam and I had a bit of a falling out, but I went to the beach with him anyway, that I dropped my phone and it smashed, that he fell over and banged his head, and we've been in A and E all night. This appeases her, and she's relieved when I tell her that Liam's dad knows. Shit. Liam's dad. What's he doing?

After I've showered and eaten a Cheezely salad sandwich, Mum and I have a cup of coffee in the kitchen, just chatting about this and that and university. She texts Dad, her phone immediately beeps, and she tells me he says *hi* and wishes Liam all the best.

I kick my feet, as they hang from the tall breakfast-bar stool and think how lucky I am to have a family like this. When I'm having a bad day, I moan to myself about how they stifle me, but, really, I know they've always got my back. Not like Chelse's mum and dad. Her dad left her mum for some slag he was having an affair with, and her mum's all broken up. Chelse says she hates being at home because of having to walk on eggshells. That's why she's always round her nan's.

Once Mum's gone to work, I decide to post a few Body Shop things on social media. I do this partly to make everything look normal, partly to keep myself busy while I wait, and partly because I don't know what else to do. Then remember I haven't got a phone. It's annoying, but I set up my laptop, put some of their new make-up range on, and do a live video of some products I'm going to give away. Everything feels unreal, but when I play the video back, I come across perfectly normal. I post the video on all my channels. That will do for today, and it's nearly ten o'clock. I ring for a taxi, go to Tesco and try to claim a new phone off my insurance. When they say that they'll deliver my new phone tomorrow, I kind of panic, saying my boyfriend is in hospital in a bad way, and I need a phone today. The girl serving me takes pity on me, and suggests that as I'm due an upgrade, I just do that. The whole thing takes bloody ages, but at least I'm up and running when I leave the shop. I sit on the benches outside and look out over the carpark. I've bought a Diet Coke and a Bounty. Screw the vegan thing – I need cheap calories right now, and some comfort, and if that means a cow's been milked, then fucking so be it. I'm trying to save my boyfriend's life here, and something's got to give. I'll try again next January.

I need to find Liam. I text him, wait fifteen minutes, but he doesn't respond. Either he's dead, or Richard has smashed his phone too. I do the only thing I can do – I walk down to Richard's flat.

Town's about as busy as it gets these days, which isn't very. When I get to Richard's black front door, there's no one around. I take my keys out and scratch *fucking* above the *cunt* that was already there. I bang on the flaking wood, but there's no answer. They must have gone. I decide to check and see if Richard's car's there, so I go round to the double doors we parked behind yesterday.

I press my head against the wood so I can peer through the gap between the doors. To my surprise, one of them gives a bit, and when I step back, it swings open. They've been pulled-to. Closed, but not locked.

Adrenalin courses through me as I step into the driveway-come-courtyard and carefully secure the doors behind me. Richard's car is not there. I go to the old wooden door that leads into the flat, hoping against hope that this hasn't been locked either. I try the handle with shaking hands. It bangs in its hinges. Locked. Fuck. I have to get into the flat! I try to kick the door down, like they do on the telly, and of course, I fail. I consider calling a lock smith, telling them I've lost my key, but I don't have the nerve – they'd probably need proof of ID, and they'll have an app that tells them who's house belongs to who, just in case. Otherwise, people would be breaking into each other's houses all the time. I look around for another entry point, then remember I was supposed to let Chelse know where I am. Fuck – what if *she s* called the police?! Oh my God, I can't cope with this. I need to get inside, so if Liam is bleeding on the floor, I can save his life. Or at least try to. I can't let him down again.

There's a small window just to the right of the door. It has that opaque glass that you get in bathroom windows so no one can see you on the toilet. Knowing it's going to be tough to break, I take off my boot and smash its heel against the glass with every ounce of strength I possess.

The glass doesn't smash, and even if it had, there's no way I would have been able to squeeze through it without cutting myself to shreds. Then I notice the lock next to the door. It's one of those ones where you punch in a certain number and get the key that's inside to get into the house. I have no idea whether there's a key in there, but I'm guessing that's how Richard used to get the key to the people who rented his flat when he was in Liverpool.

Okay. Four digits. Channel your inner Richard, Portia. Actually, don't. Repress that shit forever and ever amen. Something about the way he guessed my phone password lets me know how to crack his. Great minds think alike. I try 3466 – DINO. 5426 – LIAM. 7434 – RICH (he's a total narcissist). 2691 – BMW1. Fucking hell – I'm running out of options, and this is a longshot, anyway. Hmm. Great minds think alike. 9656 – YOLO. It couldn't be, could it? Result! Ha! Fuck you, Richard, you're no better than any of the rest of us!

You only live once. When I think about it, it does sum up Richard's approach to life. This sobers me up a bit, and I almost feel some empathy. The lock clicks open, and I step inside. The absence of life is palpable – I know there is no one here, but I also know that I'm going to check every room just to make sure. I wish I could trust my gut more – it would save so much time.

The nearest thing to life in the flat is the blood in the grouting and Noel, the stuffed seagull, in his display case. Comforted by the knowledge that Richard's not here, I force myself to look at the dead bird. I feel desperately sorry for him. Birds are meant to fly. They're meant to have the most freedom of any creature on earth. This poor bugger has had all his innards removed by some sick fuck, replaced by I have no idea what. His eyes look real, but they're probably glass. I wonder what happens to the eyes and the innards. This phrase pops into my head: *eyes are the windows to the soul.* The only window Noel has to look out of is the one he's trapped inside. I think about him, flying high above a cliff and out to sea. I wonder what he's seen. And then it hits me. When I wanted some music, what was on the first memory stick that Richard asked me to put in? Noel Gallagher's High Flying Birds. Instinctively, I know how this seagull got his name. And what does that say about Richard?!

"Okay," I say to Noel. "I can't stand around being repulsed by Richard all day. He's not here. Liam's not here. Which probably means that Liam went with Richard, or Richard took him." I pace around Richard's work room, looking at the tools and the maps. Of course! The maps! Richard took me so Liam would do what Richard wanted him to do, which was to help him discover a new species of dinosaur. He'd asked me to 'go on a little holiday 'with him to the Isle of Wight! So that's where they'll be! Also, I'm now certain that Liam's alive.

I punch the air and make to high-five Noel. I know he's dead, but I wonder if he'd appreciate some fresh air on his feathers. I take my boot off again, put my hand inside it, and smash the display case. Glass flies everywhere, but Noel stands firm. He's upright and intact, but covered in shards of glass. Grabbing one of Richard's paintbrushes, I dust Noel down. I've never really looked at a seagull before, but up close, they're beautiful. So many shades of grey and black and white. I imagine what Noel's wings would have looked like spread wide, and consider stretching them out, but I daren't. Like a butterfly, I reckon. Very gently, I pick him up and carry him to the big window in the front room. I push one of the sofas up against the window, and prop Noel up on its top so he can take in the view. I hope he can see the river.

And now I know what I have to do. I need Liam's dad's help, and I need to tell Mum that I'm staying over in hospital with Liam and hope to God she doesn't get it into her head to visit. But then she wouldn't be able to, would she? Because of Covid! But then they wouldn't let me stay, either. Fuck. I'll think of something. I'll say I'm staying over at Chelse's or something.

Fuck. I never called Chelsea! Sitting down behind Noel, I call Chelse from my new phone. She picks up on the third ring.

"Chelse. I'm okay. Liam's with Richard. I think they've gone to Isle of Wight. I'm going to get hold of Liam's dad and get him to take me there."

"Umm, Porche, I think you need to calm down a bit. How do you know they've gone to the Isle of Wight?" Chelse ends her sentence with a burp.

"Nice!" I say, laughing.

"Sorry, Porche. I've been feeling rough as hell all day. Do you need me to come with you?" Not *do you want me to come with you?*

"No, it's okay. I'm going to run down to Adam's shop now. He's self-employed – I'm sure he'll shut early."

"Yeah, of course he will. He'll want to get his boy back."

Yeah. His boy. Who might not actually be his boy.

Chelsea

I sit on the bench in town for ages after Jack's gone, just thinking about things. About what makes a person a good person. I'm just about to get up and mooch off to the bus station, when someone sits down next to me and hands me a takeaway coffee. It's the guy who won the stuffed seagull! He's still got it with him, except now it's in a big John Lewis bag so it can't see me.

"I thought you looked like a latte girl," he says, smiling.

"Thank you," I answer, taking the coffee from his outstretched hand. I sip it. It's comforting, even though it is another coffee. And I can tell it's not a skinny one, either. I'm going to enjoy this.

"Don't worry," he says, still smiling, sipping a hot drink of his own, "I'm not stalking you – I just saw you sitting there when I was on my way to John Lewis. I was in there for ages, I've walked back down this end of town and you're still here. I thought, *I ll get a Costa, and if she s still sitting there, I ll get her one too.* And here you are. Still sitting here. And you don't look happy."

His name's Richard. He walks me back to the bus stop, and tells me he lives in Eskwich, too. He's got a flat there. He's a university professor, and his girlfriend – who'd been in The Beeches – eventually committed suicide. That's why he supports mental health charities. I feel like such a fraud, and I tell him that, as we sit up on the top deck of the bus watching the white lines in the middle of the road. He tells me he's a palaeontologist. I tell him my best mate's boyfriend's hoping to do that at uni. He smiles. "There're more of us about than you'd think!" he says.

The bus pulls into Eskwich and we get off. He thanks the driver, and we walk up Memorial Lane and into town. There's no one about. "Okay, well, nice to meet you," I say. He can tell I don't really want to go home.

"Fancy a beer and a burger at 'spoons?" he says. "My treat."

I laugh, and we head off down Angel Hill together.

I remember calling my mum and telling her that I'd had such a great day that I'd met up with Portia, had a few drinks, had gone back to hers and had a few more drinks, and that I was crashing on the sofa and would be back after work the next day. She hadn't been impressed – especially seeing as I had work in the morning – but she was a mess, too, and I knew in my heart that she was only thinking of me when she said it was okay. Also, she could mope around the house and listen to Evanescence all she liked. She'd probably sink a few bottles of wine herself.

I remember Richard setting his alarm, laughing at me because I was in a state, and I had to be at work for six in the morning. He was on sabbatical, he said. That's why he was back down in Devon. I asked him which university he taught at, and I think he said Liverpool, but I can't be sure.

The alarm he'd set woke us both at five. It was still dark, and we were still drunk. I was lying on my side, and his arm was slung over me. He was lovely and warm, and he turned the alarm off, and I snuggled back into him, and we had sex. I had the nagging feeling that we'd done it before, but I'd been so drunk anything could have happened.

I woke with a jolt and reached for my phone. Five forty-two. I tried to wake Richard, but he wouldn't budge, so I found his shower, dressed, and when I came out, he was there with a coffee and some toast. We had the quickest breakfast known to man, he showed me out of his flat, and I ran up Angel Hill, past the town hall, and just made it to Costa to see Brogan disappearing through the door. As soon as I'd got in and thrown one of the spare Barista tops on, I texted Mum to let her know I'd made it to work. It was ten o'clock before I got a response.

Realising I hadn't got Richard's number, I walked down to his flat after work. When the double doors to the courtyard I remembered going into, wouldn't open, I banged on them. Nothing. I looked up at the windows that could be his flat, but I couldn't remember which way we'd gone in. Just to the left of the double doors, there was a black front door with a letterbox, but someone had scratched *cunt* into it, so it couldn't have been Richard's. And if it *had* been the door to the flat, he would have taken me in through there, rather than going through a courtyard, past a car, and in through another door. I waited on the street there for an hour, either for him to come out, or someone who lived in the flat next door to come home and let me in or give me his number. In the end I went down to 'spoons and had a beer and a burger on my own. I thought about asking the guy behind the bar if he knew the man I'd come in with last night, but I don't remember him working yesterday, and in any case, I was too embarrassed that he'd think I was a slag. I was just fucking glad that Declan had been in Milton Keynes on a course for work. I panicked and checked my phone for texts and photos, but there was nothing after I'd texted him saying I was doing some voluntary work in Exeter for a mental health charity. He'd never had a good signal from Milton Keynes, but I was a bit disappointed to find he hadn't even sent me a thumbs-up. Or a page full of Xs.

There was no response from Richard when I banged on the doors again on my way home. I tried to remember what he'd said. When had he been going back to Liverpool? It must have been today. Tears came before I could stop them, but on the walk home, I pulled myself together. We'd had a lovely night. Richard had been kinder to me than Declan had ever been, and he was probably as upset as I was that we'd forgotten to exchange numbers. It had been an impulsive and passionate one-night stand, and in the end, I was proud I'd done it. I only panicked for one second, because I'd definitely seen a packet on condoms on his bedside table. And if one or both of them had split and I'd

got caught, well, my life now had a direction. I wished I'd
got a photo of him though. He was well fit!

Liam

I've never been to the Isle of Wight before. I knew it had been Grumfer's favourite place. He'd been banging on about how he used to take Dad – Adam – there when he was a kid, ever since he'd been ill. But I'd never been. I did the trip to Skye, which was awesome - we found loads of eroded vertebrae, petrified wood and the like – but I'd never managed to get to 'Dinosaur Island'. The sun broke through the blanket of cloud, casting moody shadows onto the water. I'd had no idea the port at Southampton would be this busy, or that there would be so many yachts. I mean, what job do you have to have to be able to afford a yacht?! Images of Portia in one of her OnlyFans poses on the front of the boat, the sky a hazy, seductive blue behind her, flooded my mind. Maybe she was right. Maybe I was being a possessive misogynistic prick – what she does with her body is up to her. Guilt tugs at my stomach as I remember how I'd told her paying Stuart back would be up to her; that she was an idiot flushing the coke away, and even more of an idiot for telling him. The only idiot there had been me.

"Want to come with me, or are you just going to sit there wallowing in self-pity?" Richard knew exactly where to go and exactly what to do. He'd clearly been planning this for a while. We were going to take his car on the ferry so we could have our freedom and drive round the island when we got there. From the Solent estuary, I could make out the bulge of the island on the watery horizon.

I hung my top half over the side of the ferry and stared into the churning waves. I hoped that my hands would get splashed, dangling as they were, but they didn't because almost immediately, Richard's vice-like hands were round my waist, pulling me back to upright.

"You realise that if you go over, you'll either be sliced to bits by the propellors, or the coastguard will have pulled you out within five minutes?"

I stare at Richard. He doesn't look well. I know I wouldn't be strong enough to push him overboard; and, yeah, he was probably right about the outcome. In any case, he still hadn't told me who my real dad was.

"Are you alright?"

"I will be when we get off this fucking boat," he says. "Now, I showed your girlfriend my pictures and notes, and if we're going to be effective when we get to the Chines, you need to see them too."

Portia

Liam's dad's bike shop is mostly window. It's rammed-packed with bikes. Some are ground level, some are standing a bit higher or purpose-made shelves, some are hanging from chains, to give the impression that they're being ridden over rugged mountain terrain. They're a mix of balance bikes for toddlers, women's, men's, racing bikes, mountain bikes – there's even a tandem! In what space there is between the bikes, there're pumps, gloves, water bottles, and helmets. Liam's grandad put a string of primary-coloured lightbulbs up one Christmas about five hundred years ago when he owned the shop, and no one's taken them down, so the place looks really jolly and inviting.

And it had been, when Liam's grandad was running it. Keith had taught virtually every kid in town how to ride, and he was involved with the BMX club. I think someone said once that when he was younger, he'd done the Tour de France, but this town is renowned for its bullshit rumours, so maybe he didn't. Anyway, Keith had been a *pillar of the community* or a *national treasure* or whatever until he'd got dementia.

Even though he'd trained up Adam - Liam's dad - he refused to stop working until one day when he'd been trying to make himself a shepherd's pie for tea. His next-door neighbour heard the bang, then smelt the smoke and called all the emergency services. He saved Keith's life. And probably the lives of everyone who lived in the terrace. To boil the potatoes, Keith had put them in the kettle. He had to go into a care home after that, and it nearly broke Liam. They'd been so close. If I'm honest, he'd been closer to his 'Grumfer 'than he was to his dad.

Adam was alright. I mean, he was cool – he wasn't over-protective of Liam, and he let him make his own choices.

He let us drink cider at his house when we were like fifteen – my mum went mental when she found out! But Liam said his dad had done loads of drugs when he'd been younger and it had fucked him up, and what with Liam's mum being murdered it was kind of like he was dead inside. Liam says he just goes to work, comes home, sits in front of the telly till he falls asleep, and does it all again the next day. I know it pisses Liam off, but I kind of feel sorry for his dad. Now he knows that he might not even be Liam's dad. Head-fuck.

As I approach the shop, I can see Adam between the bikes. He's slumped over the counter with his head in his hands. There are no customers, thank God. It's not till I nearly walk into the closed door that I see he's put the 'closed 'sign up. I think this is the first time I've ever been to the shop and the door hasn't been propped open.

"Sorry, we're closed!" Adam calls through the glass of the door. He's barely raised his head.

"Adam! It's me – Portia!" I shout, my hands and face pressed up against the glass. That makes him pay attention. He twists his face towards me, but otherwise remains motionless. He glares at me. Of course, the last time I saw him, I was at the top of the stairs at Richard's. I can see the distrust in his eyes. He's slow to open the door.

"Come in, then," he says. I am not his favourite person right now. "Have you heard from Liam?"

"No. That's what I need to talk to you about!"

"Well, it would have been nice for someone to let me know he'd discharged himself from hospital, without me having to drive in there are make a twat of myself in front of the doctors and nurses! You could just see 'bad father ' written all over their faces!"

"I'm sorry, Adam, but Richard smashed my phone – he was holding me hostage – he –"

"Holding you hostage?! You were up there sharing a bloody takeaway with him! I don't know what your game is, Portia, but –"

"Adam!" I slam my fist onto the counter in a move that's painfully reminiscent of Richard. "Richard's got Liam and I know where they've gone, and you have to help me!"

Isle of Wight, January 2022

Richard

I love the sea, not least for its secrets – *sea-crets!* – and the irony of the fact that when I travel on it, I am seasick, is not lost on me. The journey from Southampton to East Cowes only takes an hour, but I know I'm not going to be right for the rest of the day. There's a smirk spreading over the fear on Liam's face, and I don't like it. I could have pushed him over the side earlier. He was hanging over the edge, despite of the pain it must have set off in his broken head, daring me to. It's a shame he's not my boy, really – it would have been poetic, the history repeating: finding out all he ever thought about his life was a lie, being betrayed by those he loves, things never quite ever working out for him … My smile would be nostalgic if it weren't for the bitterness.

"Didn't fancy the hovercraft, then? It would have been quicker!" he says, flipping through a leaflet he picked up on the ferry.

"You can't take cars on the hovercraft, *Will*iam." The ice in my tone nips that little bit of rebellion in the bud. His face falls with resignation as he pulls the car door closed.

Patchwork fields, cottages with rambling rose gardens – the Isle of Wight isn't a million miles from Devon, literally or figuratively. Despite the cold, I'm driving with the window down. It's clearing my head and easing my stomach a little, and I love the ever-present tang of salt in the air. The adrenalin is beginning to pump. It always makes me laugh that the media portray excitement as something that only occurs in cities, and that there's nothing but peace and quiet in the countryside. I've been based in Liverpool for over a decade now and nothing life-changing has ever happened to me there. Yes, there's always a bar open, a concert on, ad infinitum, but at the end of the day, it's just a greater number of people filling the streets, bigger buildings, more traffic. Humanity going about its daily grind. Mothers in false eyelashes and tracksuits pushing pushchairs round supermarkets, students with their laptops in coffee shops, old ladies in purple jackets waiting at bus stops, gym-bunnies in suits yelling into iPhones while trying not to drop their takeaway coffees. Yes, there's a *buzz,* but it's just white noise to me.

"Are we nearly there, yet?"

I snort with laughter before I can stop myself. "Why? Do you need your nappy changed or something?"

Liam glares at me, his cheeks flushed with embarrassment.

"I used to change your nappies, you know," I say, conversationally. "I was there when your mum went into labour. I helped her. I was there when you were born. Which is more than can be said for either of your so-called fathers."

"I hate you."

The words are very quiet, very deliberate. I let them fill the car. I press the button to close my window, so they can't escape. We continue the journey in silence for a few minutes.

"Yes, we are."

"What?" Liam can hardly force the word out. He really doesn't want to talk to me, but he can't help himself! I must get a grip on myself. Ah, fuck it! I laugh. Loudly.

"We're nearly there, *Will*iam! Compton Bay. We're going straight into Compton! Haha! Find it on your phone and play it, will you?"

"Find what on my phone?"

"*Straight Outta Compton.* It's a song. I think you'll like it."

Liam snorts. "Maybe I would, if you hadn't made me leave my phone behind."

This is annoying. Now the song has popped into my head, I have an overwhelming desire to hear it. It's more than a desire. I have to hear it. I pull my phone out from the compartment in the side of my door, and hand it to him.

"Really?"

"Just find the fucking song."

"What's your PIN number?"

PIN number. Words are meaningless, these days. I take a deep breath. "9656."

"9656? That's the same as Portia's! Fuck me – *YOLO*?!" He dissolves into laughter. I could kill him.

"Find. The. Fucking. Song."

And with that soundtrack, we pull up in the carpark at the top of the cliff.

Compton Bay, Isle of Wight, January 2022

Liam

It's fucking freezing, and my head is banging. I should have stayed in hospital. All I want to do is lie down. I should have called my dad. I could still call my dad – I have Richard's PIN number! Yes, he'll probably change it, but he's too wrapped up in himself at the moment. He's standing outside the car, leaning on the open door looking out to sea, with the music still blasting from his phone. He took it off me as soon as he stopped the car, but it's on the driver's seat, just an arm-stretch away. The song stops, and he's turned it off and stuffed it into his pocket before the ads kick in.

"Get out of the car, William."

"My name's *Liam*!" I shout at him. I can't help it. It takes him by surprise, and he smiles. The wind up here is fierce, and nearly knocks me sideways. My eyes prick with tears. The sky is flat and pale grey, the churning sea a dark, slate shade. The cliff tops are green, but I can't be bothered to examine which plants make up that greenery. The stretch of cliff-face jutting out into the ocean to my right is bright white but the one we're standing on is ruddy, like the soil in Devon, and I can see that the rock is just crumbling onto the sandy beach that holds the dinosaur footprints. I get that rush of adrenalin I haven't had, but have badly needed in *so* long … I glance over roof of the car, at Richard. He's grinning at me, bag in one hand, ice creams in the other. I hadn't noticed the bright yellow van. I take a *99* from him and stalk off, my back to the wind and the waves.

"Where are you going?!"

"To get a fucking Coke. Want one?"

I know it's all sugar, but I feel better after something to eat and drink. I could do with a carvery at a nice, warm pub, really, but this is as good as I'm going to get for the moment. We trudge down the steps that have been cut into the cliff just for people like us, examining the terrain as we go. *Let s go fossil-hunting, shall we, son?* Richard had said as we set off. I can't believe he really thinks that we're going to find anything worth finding – in an academic sense – at all, let alone this ground-breaking discovery he's hellbent upon.

He had the decency to lend me a waterproof jacket and some gloves, but they do little to stop the wind that's tearing in off the sea. I'm not going to be able to bend my fingers properly soon, and I'm dizzy from bending down so much. There's a box of painkillers in the car, but I'm not going to open that until I'm desperate. I try just walking about on the beach and taking in what would be a stunning coastline if the sun was out, but the sand and stones compel me to study them.

"Liam! Come over here!"

Uncle Richard's found the dinosaur footprints. He's standing on one, waving at me, laughing with glee, and when I jog over, he gets out his phone and takes a picture of his feet. He gets off, helps me up, gives his phone to me, and I do the same. We're both laughing. He takes a deep breath. I copy him, drawing as much salty air into my lungs as they'll hold. We're both inhaling history. I jump down, jarring my head, and kiss the rock, and then we sit in silence, imagining magnificent Baryonyx wading in the water. A gull shrieks from above, and Richard rests his head back in his hands and watches it rip through the sky. I think of the stuffed gull in his room of horrors, and I get it. I do get it. What are we made from? Where are we heading? What's the point of all this, anyway? It suddenly occurs to me that there doesn't have to be a point, and all I want to do now is enjoy this day. If Covid's taught us anything, it's that we could all be dead tomorrow. Maybe finding proof of the end of the dinosaurs, or finding a new species isn't the important thing, after all. Maybe the best thing I could do with my life is enjoy it. *YOLO.*

Richard and I pick our way along the base of the cliffs, chatting about his research, my PhD proposal, digs we've been on, who would win a *Celebrity Death Match* - David Attenborough or Chris Packham? It's actually great. He suggests finding a B and B before the sun goes down, and eventually agrees to a pub lunch.

I guess to an on-looker, we look like father and son.

But we're not father and son, and when he leaves his phone on the table while he goes to the loo, I pick it up and unlock it. My first thought is to call Portia, but I remember Richard smashed her phone like he smashed my head. I consider calling Dad, but he'd spend so long having a go at me for leaving hospital, and asking me what's going on, Richard would be back before I could get a word out. I could call the police, but that would put an end to the fossil-hunting for one thing, and me finding out who my real dad is, for another. Instead, I scroll through his photos.

Our feet on the dinosaur footprints. Screenshots of ferry times. A few of Portia, bruised and bloody, asleep – or unconscious - on a white bed. Selfies with groups of colleagues from the university. I glance up in the direction of the toilets. No sign of him. I scroll faster. Fossils. Shots from dig sites. As I approach the end, I recognise some pictures. He's taken shots of the old photos I found when I was going through Grumfer's stuff with Portia, before he went in the home. There's the one of Mum and Dad and they guy they rented their flat off, and their mates. There's the one of Richard and some blokes in a pub about a million years ago. Shit - that must be The Riverboat! There's Mum and a moody-looking girl, when they must have been in their early-teens, sitting in the beer garden clinking bottles of Hooch. That must have been Cathy, or whatever she was called. Yes, there's one of Richard and Cathy, arms round each other, at a barbeque. I wish I had longer to look at them – I'm trying to see if they look like they love each other, but the original photos are grainy, and I can't make out their expressions. I glance up again. Still no one, but I can hear a hand drier. And there it is. One of Mum and Dad standing outside the flat on Thomas Street, cigarettes in hand, standing very close together, clearly having a heart-to-heart. They don't know the picture's being taken. I wonder who took it. Maybe it was Richard. Anyway, the important thing is, you can tell it's Dad, because I look the spit of him. Except it's not Mum and Adam. It's the guy in the denim jacket – their landlord. What was his name again?

"His name is Will, Liam."

Portia

"So what are we going to do when we get there? I mean, I know the Isle of Wight is small, but it's not *that* bloody small!"

"They'll be down by the coast, Adam, looking for fossils!"

Liam's dad lets out a hollow laugh. "It's a fucking *island,* Portia. It's pretty much *all* coast!" He scrabbles around in the compartment under the handbrake and pulls out a flash drive. More memories of Richard. I shiver. "Turn that shit off and put this in, will you?" he says.

"It's not Noel Gallagher, is it?"

"Yeah, it is actually, how did you know?"

I can't believe it. My blood runs cold. "What?"

"What do you mean, what? Well, it's him and his brother, anyway," he says, and relief floods me as I hear the opening strains of *Rock n Roll Star.* I should have realised – we're approaching Stonehenge. Liam and his dad come here every year around the summer solstice, in memory of his mum.

"Do you want to stop?" I ask, hoping he'll say *yes.* I've been past here hundreds of times, but I've never stopped and got out to look at the stones properly. I'm going to university to study history, for fuck's sake – I really should have been to Stonehenge by now.

"No. I just want to get to the Isle of fucking Wight and get my son back!" It's a fair point, but knowing that Richard wants Liam to help him, and so will be looking after him and keeping him safe, kind of takes the edge off the urgency of the mission.

Adam cracks open the can of Red Bull that's been sitting in the cupholder since we left Eskwich. It must be warm. "Want some?"

"Umm, no thanks. I'll stick to my water. Thanks."

Adam chucks his phone onto my lap. "My card's in the pocket bit of the case. Book us some ferry tickets. And a B and B."

Definitely Maybe plays in no particular order all the way to Southampton, and then all the way from the boat to Brighstone. It's pitch black outside now, and still freezing cold, and all I want to do is sleep. Adam walks up to the beautifully warm and welcoming bar in The Three Bishops, holding his facemask just in case, and orders us drinks and something to eat. We flop into the booth at the back. I'm asleep before the food arrives.

"You eat like a pig, Portia!"
"Oh, well, cheers, Adam, thanks for that! I'm bloody starving!" I retort but make a point of slowing down a bit.

We're back in the bar for breakfast the next morning, tucking into our fry-ups, in the booth again, this time with Adam on the soft seat, which means he has his back to the bar and when I glance up from my plate to sip my coffee, I see them.

I freeze, but Adam's intent on his breakfast and doesn't notice. Richard and Liam have just come down from the rooms upstairs and are standing at the bar! Richard's talking to the guy who brought our breakfast over; Liam's leaning against one of the pillars, rolling a cigarette.

"Does Richard know what car you've got?"

"What?" Adam asks, shoving another forkful of fried egg into his gob.

"You heard!" I hiss.

"Speak up, girl! I can't hear you!" he laughs.

"Adam! Shut the fuck up!" I spit, nodding in the direction of Richard and Liam who are just walking out of the pub and out of sight.

Adam jumps up, but can't extricate himself from the

table, so just shouts "Oi!" but it's too late, they're gone and I'm glad.

"Adam! Shut up! We've got to follow them!" I grab my bag, rush over to the guy behind the bar, thank him for breakfast and apologise for the mess, telling him we've got to run, literally, by which time Adam is behind me, pushing me out of the door and into the beer garden, just in time to see a black BMW disappearing round the corner to the right.

"Get in the car!" Adam shouts, and he's pulling away before I've even got the door shut.

"Do you think Liam saw your car?" I say, breathlessly.

"Well, if he didn't, his head's worse than we thought," Adam says, swinging the battered estate onto New Road, then flooring it.

"Stay back, Adam!" I say, trying to get my seatbelt into its hole.

"What for?!" he counters, "The road's straight and there's no one else on it. If they've seen us, they've seen us!" He pauses. "And anyway, it doesn't matter if they've seen us because as soon as I get close enough, I'm ripping that bastard's head off!"

"Adam, he's your brother!"

"Only by blood."

At a T–junction we follow Richard's BMW and turn right. We are – I don't know – about three or four car lengths behind them. Adam is sitting bolt upright in his seat, his knuckles white on the wheel. I'm gripping my seatbelt with both hands, forcing my body as far back into my seat as it will go, my feet stretched out and pressed to the floor in a pathetic parody of braking – Adam changes down to second gear and the estate jolts and roars - I think Adam's going to try to ram Richard off the road!

"Adam!" I scream, automatically bracing myself for impact, but the sleek, black car suddenly pulls away from us. Adam's got his foot flat on the floor. "Adam!" I shout again. The BMW is swerving all over the road, and I can see Liam's bandaged head being thrown about.

"Bastard!" Adam yells, hammering his hands on the steering wheel. The low hedges on either side of the road become a green smudge and I think the engine will blow up before we crash and then suddenly red lights! Richard's braking – Adam can't react in time – I shut my eyes – Adam screams "LIAM!" – but there's no impact – Richard's yanked his car off the road somehow and we flash past, Adam shouting "Fuck! Fuck! Fuck!" and then there's the jolt and I feel the seatbelt slice into my neck, and I'm thrown forwards as Adam brakes, but again – no impact – no airbag – and I'm slammed back into my seat and Adam's doing a three-point turn in the road and we race back up to where Richard's car disappeared.

Adam pulls up slowly. He doesn't turn into the carpark – he brings us up alongside it, blocking the road. Painfully, I turn my neck. Adam's grey top is soaked through with sweat, defining his biceps and the thick veins of his arms. His face, like mine, is turned to where Richard's car has stopped, right in the centre of the carpark. There are no other cars there, and thank God there are and were no other cars on the road! I look at the clock on Adam's dash – it's not yet eight o'clock in the morning. Adam turns to meet my eyes. His face is pale, sweating and flushed all at the same time.

"You okay?" he murmurs.

"Yes."

Adam nods, puts the car in gear and swings into the carpark. Parking a few spaces away from Richard's car, Adam slowly opens his door and climbs out. I follow suit, and scan the area. "They must be in the car."

Hesitantly, we walk over, as if Richard's Beemer was full of explosives that could go off at any second. Approaching from the side, we can't see into the back windows as they're blacked out, and there's seemingly no one in the front, either, but then they could have ducked down, or left the vehicle, or be hiding round the other side of it –

"What's that noise?"

I hold my breath and try to ignore the pounding of my blood in my ears, and we both freeze and listen. On top of the gale that's blowing, and the crashing waves, we can hear voices. I can't make out exactly what's being said, but it's unmistakably an argument. I look at Adam, searching his face. His shoulders drop, the tension draining from them. He walks all the way around the car. He puts his face up against the windows.

"It's them," he says. "They're on the beach."

We make our way to the cliff edge. "Adam –"

"What's the matter?"

"I'm scared of heights."

"Fuck's sake," he mumbles, taking the few paces back towards me and gently taking my hand. I've never stood on the edge of a cliff before. The wind's so powerful I'm afraid it will blow us both into the sea. Adam's top whips around his body, and I let go of his hand to pull my cardigan tighter around me. On a nice day, this would be beautiful; today it just feels austere, unforgiving. To my right, bare, white cliffs stark as bone, cut into the ocean. The water and sky meet at the horizon in a cold, grey line; white-crested waves smash onto reddish sand. And there's the shouting again, the sound carried by the wind, from our left.

Adam pulls me off in that direction, and we come to the crude, steep steps that will take us onto the beach. Adam goes first, gripping the freezing metal banister, and I follow his trainers until we touch the sand.

The beach seems narrower, now we're on it, the waves taller. As for the cliffs, I'm more scared standing at their base than I was standing on the grass on top of them.

They're crumbling. Like, I stand and watch as fragments of rock trickle down in the wind. It's bloody dangerous, but it's no wonder fossil-hunters love this place so much.

"There they are."

Adam gestures to his left, and I can see the silhouettes of Liam and Richard bending together, tapping and brushing together, working intently – frantically - at the cliff face, on a mound of rocks.

"Be careful!"

"I'm fucking trying to! If you'd have checked the tide times –"

"I'm the one that got us here! I'm the one who spotted it! I make one fucking mistake and that's all anyone remembers! Story of my fucking life! Just get on with it! And BE CAREFUL!"

"We shouldn't even be doing this! We should register the find, take photos, come back when it's safe – come back with a team! - and do it properly! –"

" Adam!"

I startle Liam and Richard with my cry, and they whip round to see Adam sprinting across the damp sand, over to them.

"Liam!" he shouts, his voice breaking with fear and desperation.

"Dad! I'm okay! We've just found something! Don't!"

Richard launches himself off the rocks to confront his brother, and Adam slams into him. They thump down on the sand, Adam on top of Richard, Adam pulls his arm back and then there's a wet crunch as Richard's nose breaks. As I rush over and grab Liam's hand, Richard throws his brother off him, and pulls himself upright, chuckling. Adam recovers and stands, braced to hit him again, but Liam shouts, "Dad! No! Please don't! We've found something important!"

Richard stands, spits, and wipes his mouth. He regards his hand after he does so, still laughing to himself. He shows Adam the back of his hand. "Congratulations!" he says, smiling, "This time you made me bleed!"

"Is this a fucking joke to you?!" Adam's voice cracks, and he reaches out to Liam, who grabs his arm and pulls us back, so the three of us stand together.

"Well, it was a bit of excitement for you, wasn't it, brother? A car chase! Gets the old blood pumping a bit, doesn't it?! Makes you feel alive!" Richard takes a deep breath and stretches out his arms. Adam jerks towards him, but Liam pulls him back.

"We don't have time for this shit, Richard! We need to take some photos, ring the uni, register the find, and get the fuck off this beach!"

"No! We are getting these fossils out right now! No one's going to take what's rightfully mine from me ever again! Now let go of Daddy's hand and get back to work!"

"We're not going to get them out, Richard! There isn't time!"

"STOP TALKING AND JUST DO IT!" Richard screams at Liam, his face red and furious, eye wild. He grabs Liam's arm and yanks him away from me and Adam, pulling him back to where they've been working.

"This is INSANE Richard!" But Liam picks up a hammer and some kind of chisel and resumes work. He winces. His head must be killing him. Adam is at his son's side, pleading with him, tugging at the waterproof coat he's wearing. Liam glances at his father.

"Dad – look – I know – this is all fucked up – it's really, really fucked up – but look! Look, Dad. Two jaws locked together! They were fighting!"

Liam's tone compels us to look. At first, I don't know what I'm looking at, other than a pile of stones, but Liam sweeps away some dust with a paintbrush, and traces the line of what is clearly a long jaw, filled with - "Oh my God, are those *teeth*?!"

"Yes, Miss Piggy, they are," Richard says. Without

taking his eyes from the task in hand, he starts explaining to us about the spinosaurids found somewhere on the island not long ago, and as he warms to his subject, his tone loses its aggression and gains excitement, joy even. This is how he must be in the lecture theatre. He's absorbing. This is fascinating! I look at his face, losing track of the words. He looks about twenty years younger. *Serra - toe -soo – chops Infer – oh – dious* or the *hell heron* – did he say that's what these bones are? He's talking to Liam, looking at the notebook he showed me – he's smiling – grinning – Liam's frowning, glancing at the sea – Richard's staring at the fossil they've found – he's almost jumping up and down – Liam's telling him to calm down, that we need to get off the beach before we get cut off, that they need to get some proper tools in or they'll damage the fossils, that they need to register the find, they can't do this alone, that this is insane, that it'll take years of study, probably, to work out if the dinosaurs they've found are of the same species, let alone if one or both of them are a new species, but Richard's shouting *shut up! Shut up!* that he's given Liam his PhD proposal now, and Liam's yelling that he doesn't give a fuck about finding a new species, but Richard hasn't heard him because he's coming up with potential names for the dinosaur if it is a new species, like 'Richardus Infer – oh – dious Oasis', and Liam's stopped working, he's jumped down, he's laughing, saying *fuck s sake, Richard, we may as well call it Liamosaurus or Gallagherosaurus or Scallyosaurus* and that's when something snaps in Richard and he's off the rocks too, and he punches Liam in the face, shouting "This isn't a fucking joke! I wasn't fucking joking! I'm not a fucking joke!"

Liam is down on the floor and Richard is about to stamp on his chest and my throat is raw and Adam has ripped Richard away from Liam and has him pinned against the crumbling cliff face and is smashing him again and again in the side of the head with a rock, and I scream "Adam!

No!" and Adam lets his brother fall onto the rocks and I'm at Liam's side and Adam is passing me Richard's phone with cold, fumbling hands, shouting at me to call an ambulance, but I don't know his PIN, and Liam's eyes are open and he's saying something but I can't make it out and then he grabs my hand and squeezes it tight and pulls himself up a bit and staring into my eyes he says "Yolo. Richard's PIN number. Like yours. YOLO."

"Portia. Stop crying. You have to be strong now. Like, literally."

"But there's no signal!" I let the tears fall, lean over Liam's prone body, let the sobs wrack me.

"I know. That's why you've got to help me get him up to the top of the cliff. The tide's coming in!"

I glance behind me and am shocked by the proximity of the crashing waves. Spray from a braker hits my face and I taste the salt. "Fuck!"

We're not that far from the steps we climbed down, but the beach is one hell of a lot narrower now, and in places the waves reach the cliff face.

Adam bends over his son. "Can you feel a pulse?"

"I can't feel anything, my hands are too numb!"

"Put your cheek by his nose – can you feel breath?"

"I don't know, Adam!" I'm crying again. "I'm too fucking cold!"

"Fucking hell." Adam looks at Liam. "Lee! Lee!" he whispers, "You have to wake up! You have to wake up – I've brought Grumfer's ashes! We can scatter them here, like he wanted! Lee!" Adam stops shaking his son's shoulder and wipes his eyes. His face kind of clenches, and he gets to his feet saying, "Good job you're a skinny fucker, *Bony*." Then he drags Liam up and chucks him over his shoulder like he was a sack of spuds. "Come on, Portia," he says.

"What about Richard?"

I turn back to where we left him, slumped on the rocks.

"There's no time, Portia."

"He might be dead!"

"Portia!" Adam is heading off towards the steps. I hesitate. "You couldn't feel Liam's breath – how do you think you're going to feel *his*?"

"Adam! We can't leave him!" I'm running after him now – in a minute, I'll be splashing through the surf.

"Are you going to carry him?!" Adam's started up the steps, grunting under Liam's weight.

I stop, my left foot on the bottom step. That's why they'd gone down to the beach and left me and Adam to faff about in fear by Richard's car - they'd known they didn't have much time before the tide came in. That's why there were no dog-walkers, or joggers or anything – it was not quite light, and the tide was coming in. They must have found the fossils yesterday. Oh my God – they did it. Richard did it! He found what he was looking for! He got what he always wanted! I'm so happy for him, I start crying again. This is crazy! Is this what Stockholm Syndrome looks like? I don't know what I feel, only that it's all-encompassing. I look at Richard's body, collapsed and battered on the rocks. He must be dead – he hasn't moved. I can't see clearly for the tears and the sea spray, but I imagine his blood running over the fossilised bones of his dinosaur. What a strange, secret man you are, Richard!

"Portia! Fucking come on!"

Chelsea

The early trick-or-treaters are out and about by the time I get to Nan's – groups of mums and dads holding onto whooping, laughing small children, pushing prams and buggies. I have to stop at the start of Nan's path to let a mum, Spiderman and a sparkly witch go by, the kids 'fists full of Haribos.

I laugh, and the mother says, "Soon be your turn, love!" as she passes me by and the family turn to Mrs Morrell's house. I rub my swollen, pregnant belly, and smile to myself as my baby tries to kick my hands. I was in a mess for ages because I don't know if the father is Declan or Richard, but now I don't care. It's *my* baby – *he s* my baby - and I love him, and I can't wait to go trick-or-treating with him!

Mrs Morrell *could* have made her garden hellish. The teenagers would have loved that. But she hasn't. She's put white fairy lights round all the big statues, and bowls of pinecones and apples at their feet. Or paws. Two big pumpkins, carved into the silhouettes of cats on a fence gazing at the moon, adorn the entrance to her garden, with another two on either side of her front door.

The witch knocks. The hall light comes on, making the girl's hat sparkle gold. Mrs Morrell opens the door wide, with a cheery *Hello!* and then jumps in mock-terror. The children laugh *trick-or-treat, trick-or-treat* and Mrs Morrell pulls a mixing bowl full of sweets from behind her back. The children gasp. *Just one each,* their mother warns, *there will be lots of children knocking on the lady s door tonight!* The witch and Spiderman do as they're told, and because they haven't been greedy, Mrs Morrell says they can choose another one each – *if that s okay with mum.*

When they've gone, Nan steps out and asks her neighbour in to have a cup of tea with us. "Oh, no thank you, Mrs Walker, I'd better stay here and hold the fort! But it was nice to see you, Chelsea, and we'll catch up again before the Christmas street-collection. And I'm glad you and Jack managed to work things out." She pauses, and I blush.

"I'm so sorry, again, Mrs Morrell," I say, cringing.

She laughs. "You don't need to be, love! Taxidermy does make some people a bit queasy, but it's no different from what the embalmers do to us when we die. People want to remember their loved ones as they were when they were alive. In God's image. I do the same for the dead animals I come across. I spent my working life fixing them up when I was a vet, now I restore them to their former glory so people can learn from them, in museums. I'd never do a head-on-the-wall thing – that's disrespectful. And those I can't patch up, well, they deserve a grave like any of the rest of us. We're all God's creatures, you know!"

"I know. I still think it's a *bit* gross, though." I rub my belly again, and my baby flutters in response.

Mrs Morrell chuckles. "That's okay, love. It takes all sorts, you know! And I didn't really mean for the seagull to end up in the tombola! He must have been next to the box when Jack was loading up the prizes! Still, his life ended up making money for the psychiatric unit – he didn't just rot on the side of the road. And he found someone who loves him! It couldn't have turned out better, really!"

She's right, so we all laugh. "Like you said, it takes all sorts!" Nan says, moving inside. "Come on in out of the cold, love," she says to me, "and enjoy the rest of your evening, Mrs Morrell!"

"I will," Nan's neighbour replies, turning away. "Oh, Chelsea, love?"

"Yes?"

"I just wondered if you and your partner had decided on a name for the little one, yet?"

"We have actually," I say, bashful, looking at Nan.

She beams back at me. "Oooh! Go on then!" she says, clasping her hands in expectation. I hesitate. "Oh goodness," she says. "You're not going to call him *Leaf* or *Kettle* or something bonkers like that, are you?" She pauses. "Because if you are, that's fine – he's your child, and I will love him regardless – I'm just thinking about how it would work with your surname, that's all …" Nan trails off, and I laugh.

"*Kettle*?! Oh, Nan, you do make me laugh! No, we've decided on *Richard,* actually. *Richey* for short."

Nan's smiles the warmest smile I've ever seen. "After your Grandad. Oh, love, that is so, so … I need a tissue!" She rushes inside.

"*Richard.* That's a good, strong name, Chelsea. Your grandad will be bursting with pride."

"Don't – you'll have me in tears next!"

Some more trick-or-treaters are coming up the hill, making ghost noises at each other, and jumping out of the bushes to scare their grown-ups.

"Well, I'd best get back to my post!" Mrs Morrell laughs. "Funnily enough, love, *Richard* is my nephew's name. Or great-nephew. I can never work it out – we're all related to each other somehow, aren't we?! He was the one who taught me my ' …gross' … skill! Lovely lad, but very deep. Always had an old head on his shoulders. Loved dinosaurs when he was a boy, and now he's a professor of palaeontology at a university! I've not heard from him in a while – perhaps I'll give him a ring."

As she closes the door behind her my blood runs cold. From deep inside me, Richard kicks.